THE

Tanya Landman is the author of many books for children, including *Waking Merlin* and *Merlin's Apprentice* and the Flotsam and Jetsam series. *The Kraken Snores* is the sequel to *The World's Bellybutton*, also featuring William Popidopolis and Zeus the swan. Tanya says, "I love *The Odyssey* and one morning I began to wonder what had happened to all the gods and monsters that Odysseus met. Where are they now? What are they doing? *The Kraken Snores* is the result."

Tanya is the author of two novels for teenagers, *Apache* and *The Goldsmith's Daughter*. Since 1992, she has been part of Storybox Theatre, working as a writer, administrator and performer – a job which has taken her to festivals all over the world. She lives with her family in Devon.

You can find out more about Tanya Landman and her books by visiting her website at www.tanyalandman.com

Books by the same author

THE
KRAKEN
SNORES

TANYA LANDMAN

ILLUSTRATED BY

ROSS COLLINS

WALKER
BOOKS

This is a work of fiction. Names, characters, places and incidents
are either the product of the author's imagination or, if real, are used
fictitiously. All statements, activities, stunts, descriptions, information
and material of any other kind contained herein are included
for entertainment purposes only and should not be relied on
for accuracy or replicated as they may result in injury.

First published 2008 by Walker Books Ltd
87 Vauxhall Walk, London SE11 5HJ

2 4 6 8 10 9 7 5 3 1

Text © 2008 Tanya Landman
Illustrations © 2008 Ross Collins

The right of Tanya Landman and Ross Collins to be identified as author
and illustrator respectively of this work has been asserted by them in
accordance with the Copyright, Designs and Patents Act 1988

This book has been typeset in Stempel Schneidler and Times

Printed in the UK by CPI Bookmarque, Croydon, CR0 4TD

British Library Cataloguing in Publication Data:
a catalogue record for this book
is available from the British Library

ISBN 978-1-4063-0706-1

www.walkerbooks.co.uk

For Isaac and Jack
(editing supremos)

THE SUNBURNT SWAN

When there was a blinding flash, and all the light bulbs in the house exploded at the same time, William Popidopolis thought it must be the result of his mum's dodgy DIY.

When his teacher had difficulty remembering his pupils' names, William imagined he was just stressed out about the school trip.

When the coach driver forgot her way around the streets of Brighton, William assumed she was either new to the job or having an off day.

It wasn't until later – when the bald, sunburnt swan waddled across the floor of the museum and started talking to him – that William realized something very strange was going on.

*　　*　　*

It was Monday morning. William woke up, groaned and stuck his head back under the pillow. Then he remembered his school trip to the museum. The special exhibition "From the Mud to the Stars" was no dull educational display. With evolution as its theme, it had 3D films of the first amoeba, life-sized animated dinosaurs and a rocket simulator. He was looking forward to it.

William flung aside his duvet, sat up and looked at his alarm clock. Seven o'clock. Sunny day. Time to get going. He dressed, gave his mum a shout and was answered by her usual morning wail: "Coffeeeeee..." came the pleading cry. "Pleeeee-eease ... neeeeeed coffeeeeeeee, Wiiiiiiiiill..."

William's mum wasn't like other mums. She treated him more like a friend than a son, insisted he call her Kate and dyed her hair pink whenever the mood took her. She had been a single parent for most of his ten-year-old life. William hadn't known his dad at all, until one day last spring when Nikos Popidopolis – owner of the only tav-erna on the tiny Greek island of Spitflos, and William's father – had invited him and Kate to stay. But William had found a lot more waiting for him in Spitflos than just his long-lost father. Zeus, king of the gods, had desperately needed his help. Together they had flown to the Underworld to meet Odysseus (who turned out to be William's distant ancestor), ridden on Pegasus, tricked two Gorgons into petrifying each other and saved the world. Not bad, for a week's work.

Things had seemed a little dull since they'd returned home. True, his school work had got a lot easier. He felt more on top of things. The trouble was, his teachers hadn't quite adjusted to William's new-found confidence. He was asking so many questions that they had started to suspect that he was trying to wind them up. Earlier in the term, his class had been doing a project on electricity and experimenting with what it could pass through and what it couldn't. William was fascinated.

"*Why* does it go through metal? Why not wood? Or plastic?"

He asked question after question, until Mr Cox confessed irritably, "I don't know why, William! It just does, OK? Can we all go home now?"

Then there had been the art lesson when they were supposed to draw pictures of what they'd done in their holidays. William produced a long strip cartoon featuring snake-haired monsters and a multi-headed dog. His art teacher – who had once written on William's school report that he was "a bit lacking in the ideas department" – laid a hand carefully on his shoulder as if he were a ticking time bomb and said, "Hmmm, time to rein in the imagination a little, I think. You need to focus more on the real world."

All in all, school was OK – it was certainly better than it had ever been before. But finally grasping the nine times table wasn't as thrilling as leaping onto a flying horse in heroic fashion. By the time of the museum outing, he was desperate to escape the confines of the classroom.

William thudded down the stairs two at a time and boiled the kettle while he ate cereal and drank orange juice. Then he made his mum a cup of super strong coffee to wake her up, and carried it into her bedroom. Her pink cropped hair poked up from beneath the duvet like the quills of a very embarrassed hedgehog. The rest of her was curled into a tight ball. William fanned the mug, wafting coffee fumes in her direction until a hand appeared, sticking bolt upright and swivelling towards him like the periscope of a submarine. William placed the mug against her palm, watched her fingers curl possessively around it and then went off to brush his teeth.

Running his toothbrush under the tap he gave it a squirt of paste. Bit dark in here, he thought, reaching for the light switch. He pulled the string at exactly the same time as he lifted his toothbrush to his mouth. But before it could touch his lips, there was a sudden, blinding flash, a loud crack, and William was showered with broken glass.

He dropped his toothbrush and stood still, too scared to move. Blinking, he assessed the damage. He couldn't feel any blood trickling out from anywhere. No body parts had been sliced off. As far as he could tell, he'd escaped unhurt. Not that he could check himself in the mirror – that had been broken in the blast, along with the bathroom window.

William looked accusingly at the shattered spotlights above his head. Wires poked out, blackly smouldering, smelling of burnt rubber. His mum had fitted them yesterday, working late into the night to get the job done. He'd offered to help her several times. "I know about electricity," he'd said. "We did it at school." But Kate, who also hadn't quite come to terms with the new, confident William, had refused his help.

And now look what she'd done! "Some people shouldn't be allowed near a tool kit," he muttered crossly. "She could have killed me." Gingerly picking fragments of glass from his curling copper hair, William crunched across the bathroom floor.

When he opened the door he realized the disaster area wasn't confined to the bathroom. The landing light had exploded too, as well as the one in his mum's bedroom. Kate was sitting up in bed looking at the splintered glass that was sprinkled over the duvet, glittering prettily in the early morning sun.

"You've blown the whole circuit!" William said accusingly.

"Have I really?" said his mum. Her tone was slightly detached, as if she was discussing the weather with a stranger at a bus stop.

William didn't notice. "Yes," he growled. "We're lucky the house didn't catch fire!"

"Are we?" she asked politely.

"It could have been awful!"

"Really? Oh dear…"

If William hadn't been quite so absorbed with the trip to the museum, he might have wondered why his mum hadn't moved. Her usual reaction to a domestic problem – if the Hoover went wrong or the sink got blocked – was to launch herself at it, arms flailing, and beat the offending item into submission. And yet here she was, empty coffee cup in one hand, staring at the broken glass as if entranced by it, making no attempt to do anything.

"It will take ages to clear up," William complained.

"Ages…" echoed Kate.

"And then you'll have to call an electrician out. A proper one."

"Proper one…" said his mum vaguely.

"I expect it'll take hours."

"Hours…"

"You'll be hanging around all day getting it sorted."

"Sorted…"

"You won't be able to go to work."

"I won't be able to go to work," his mum agreed. She stared at her bed, frowning. There was a pause and her eyes narrowed as she asked, puzzled, "Will you?"

"Me? Yeah, I'm off to school. I'd stay and help, but I'm late enough as it is. See you later, Kate."

"Kate," she said softly to herself. "I'm Kate. That's it." She called to William's departing back, "And who are you?"

But William didn't hear.

If he hadn't been in such a rush, he might have looked out of his bedroom window. He might have wondered why the windows of the houses opposite were dark, as though their light bulbs had

also blown. He might have observed that next door's greenhouse had shattered into a million tiny pieces. He'd certainly have noticed the small white owl flying in excited circles around the head of a winged horse that was standing beside the wreckage. And he'd very definitely have recognized the bald swan that sat upon the horse's back.

But William didn't look. He had to get to school. Without a backward glance, he hurried out, slamming the front door behind him.

Mr Cox was having great difficulty with the register.

He called Amisha Patel's name three times before he finally remembered to put a tick beside it and moved on to the next one. When he got to William, Mr Cox seemed to lose it completely.

"William Popi … poopy … dopi … droopy … dopodop…" He drew in a deep breath and galloped at the name as if he was a racehorse approaching a particularly tricky fence. "Popidopi-poopydroopyopolis."

"Yes," said William through gritted teeth, expecting to hear laughter and jeers from his classmates. They usually found his name hilarious even when it was pronounced properly. But not today: most of them were staring out of the window as if they hadn't heard.

When Mr Cox got to the end of the register, he closed it with relief and emitted a huge sigh as if he'd accomplished an immensely difficult task. Then he just sat there, uncertain of what to do next.

"Hadn't we better go now?" asked William.

"Had we?"

"Yes … the coach will be waiting."

"Will it?"

William stood up. He wasn't missing a go on the rocket simulator even if his teacher was losing his marbles. "Yes," he said firmly. "Come on."

Mr Cox and the rest of the class trooped obediently out of the classroom behind William. But there was no coach outside.

"Great," growled an exasperated William. "Bang goes the museum."

Mr Cox's eyes widened for a moment. "*Does* it? Good heavens!"

"Well, yes," said William. "I mean, if we can't even get there…"

At that moment, the coach pulled up.

William hadn't noticed Kate's unusual vagueness, and Mr Cox's behaviour had irritated rather than alarmed him. The coach driver was something else.

The vehicle stopped with no problem, but then the driver sat staring at the road ahead as if she'd never seen it before. William had to bang on the doors to get her to open them. He herded his class-mates aboard like an enthusiastic border collie, and then said, "Museum, please."

The driver replied, "Where?"

"The museum."

"The museum... Yeah... OK..." The driver inhaled deeply as though girding herself for a dangerous mission, and wiped her palms on her trouser legs. She gripped the steering wheel. Then she turned to William and said, "Sorry ... I can't seem to ... I don't suppose... Can you tell me how to get there?"

In the end, William had to sit behind her, giving directions. But he was used to walking everywhere and didn't know about the one-way system. He managed to send the coach in completely the wrong direction, but no one seemed to mind. In fact, no one seemed to notice. It was probably just as well. When they reached a large roundabout William was so distracted by the sight of a red mini – going round and round at high speed as if its driver didn't know how to get off – that he didn't choose his words very carefully.

"You go straight across here," he said. The driver took him literally, steering in a dead straight line through the neatly planted floral display in the middle of the roundabout.

William was very relieved when they finally reached the museum.

"This is it! You can stop here." The coach screeched to a dramatic halt in the middle of the road.

William unfastened his seatbelt and stepped shakily onto the pavement. No one followed. Instead of running, shrieking excitedly, up the museum steps like any normal school party, his classmates remained strapped in their seats, staring vaguely out of the windows.

William was now thoroughly unsettled but, not knowing what else to do, made his way alone towards the museum entrance. The man on the door was gazing into his cup of tea and didn't look at William as he pushed his way through.

It was all very peculiar. But still, he was here now. He supposed he might as well enjoy it. It looked like he was going to be first in the queue for the rocket simulator, at any rate.

William wasn't just the first person in the queue for the rocket simulator, he was the *only* person in the queue. The museum was strangely empty and eerily quiet. Huge mechanical dinosaurs stood motionless, deprived of the electricity to power their roars because the staff seemed to have forgotten to plug them in. William wandered past displays that should have been beeping and flashing, past televisions showing nothing but his reflection on their blank screens.

When he reached the rocket simulator, William stretched over and switched it on. It blared noisily in the deserted museum. Shrugging his shoulders, William climbed in. He had three stomach-churning rides, one after the other, because he couldn't think what else to do. But there was only so much flying to the moon and back that he could manage before he started to feel queasy. He didn't want to go back to the coach – it was too peculiar – so he decided to explore the rest of the museum.

Upstairs, William noticed a plastic boat bobbing at the top of a glass tube of water. A big red button told him to PRESS HERE. William obliged. A whoosh of air, and instantly the water in the tube was filled with bubbles. When they neared the surface, much to William's surprise, the plastic boat sank to the bottom.

William was intrigued enough to read the label beneath. It explained how the stream of bubbles decreased the density of the water, thinning it so that anything floating on the surface would sink. He watched as the bubbles popped, and then, slowly, the boat rose back to the surface. He pressed the button again,

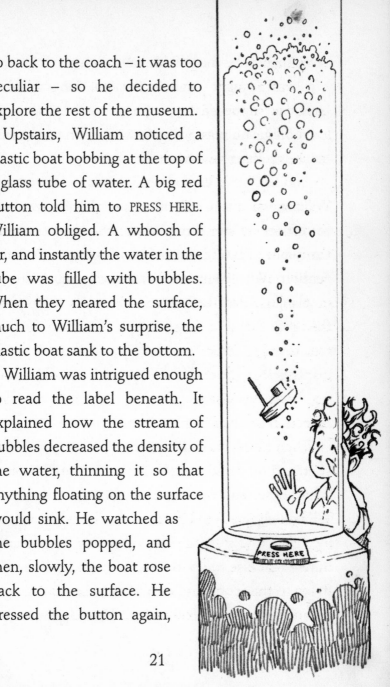

21

and the same thing happened. It was then that William caught sight of something familiar reflected in the glass.

A bald, sunburnt swan was waddling across the museum floor towards him.

Suddenly the exploding light bulbs, his mum's vagueness, Mr Cox's amnesia, the no-sense-of-direction coach driver and the absent-minded museum staff all made sense. Tingling with anticipation, William turned to face the swan.

"Hello, Zeus," he said.

THE KRAKEN

It was indeed Zeus, king of the Greek gods, who was waddling towards William on his webbed feet. He had been stuck in the shape of a swan ever since his jealous wife, Hera, had destroyed his collection of alternative bodies. He'd lost all his feathers when he'd been partially petrified by the Gorgons that William had defeated. William noticed that new ones were budding up like pimples beneath his sunburnt skin: the king of the gods looked as though he had a severe case of acne.

"What are you doing here?" asked William, smiling.

"What am *I* doing here?" the swan spluttered crossly by way of a greeting. "What are *you* doing here? I threw one of my best lightning bolts at your house and you didn't even glance out of the window. Off out of the door without a thought. We've had a terrible time tracking you down. Chased every coach in Brighton. Didn't it occur to you we might be here?"

"Well ... no," confessed William, somewhat embarrassed by his slowness. "But it's not every day a god lands in your garden."

Zeus relented. "No, I suppose not." There was a slight pause and then he said, "I managed to stop you brushing your teeth at any rate. Just as well. One drop of that water and you'd have been useless. You haven't drunk anything, have you?"

"Only orange juice," said William. "Why? Did you do something to the taps?" He suspected he already knew the answer.

"Little dash of Lethe water in the reservoir, that's all," said Zeus.

The Lethe, thought William, the river of

24

forgetfulness. No wonder everyone was looking so dazed. It was the second time Zeus had zapped his mum's memory with a dose of the stuff: he hoped the effect wouldn't be permanent.

"How much did you use?" he asked, frowning.

"A litre or so. Should only last a week."

"A week?" said William, aghast at the idea of everyone in Brighton wandering around not knowing who they were for so long. "How are people going to manage? Will they remember to eat?"

"Yes, yes, yes," said Zeus impatiently. "Never mind that, I'm sure they'll cope. The important thing is to buy us enough time to sort the current problem."

"The current problem," echoed William. Of course there was bound to be a problem. Zeus wouldn't just pop over from Mount Olympus for a casual visit. "Go on, then," he said, sitting on the floor, leaning back against the glass tube. "Tell me what's happening."

Zeus sat opposite William, his webbed feet poking out in front of him. There was a lengthy silence while the god considered where to begin. "Know much about sea monsters?" he asked suddenly.

"Er ... no," said William.

"Pity," murmured Zeus. "Neither do I." There was another pause, which this time William interrupted.

"So it's a sea monster, is it – this new problem?"

"Indeed."

William gulped. He was quite a good swimmer – he'd had a great time diving off his dad's boat into the clear turquoise waters of the Mediterranean when he was on holiday. But the idea of something large lurking in the depths was enough to give him nightmares.

"Not just any old sea monster, either," added Zeus. "The biggest. The mightiest. Poseidon's very best."

"Poseidon? Who's Poseidon?"

"My brother," answered Zeus. "King of the Sea, Protector of the Deep, Controller of the Waves, and unfortunately, the least helpful god you're ever likely to meet."

"OK," said William. "So where is it then, this monster?"

"Moving north," replied Zeus gloomily. "At its current rate it will reach British waters by the end of the week. It will be in the Channel by Friday."

"And what does it do? Attack ships and stuff?"

"That, certainly, is a feature of its behaviour."

"So we need to stop all the boats and ferries, do we?" It would be difficult, thought William. Difficult: but not impossible. He started to turn over ideas in his mind. Zeus could throw around a few thunderbolts. If he made it stormy enough, no ships would set sail.

But Zeus interrupted his flow of thoughts. "Sadly, William, there's a very great deal more than shipping under threat."

"Oh," said William, his heart sinking. "Tell me the worst."

Zeus drew in a deep breath. "I believe the monster usually lives in the warm seas of the Atlantic, somewhere near Bermuda."

"Bermuda?" asked William. "What, like in the Triangle?"

"What's that?"

"The Bermuda Triangle? It's where planes and ships and things just disappear."

"Yes, well, that sounds like the monster. I gather it's been known to snack on the odd ship or low-flying plane."

"That explains a lot," said William.

Zeus continued. "Unfortunately, every thousand years or so, the creature likes to settle down for a long sleep, and for that it likes to be in cooler water. Last time it came north it got spotted by a bunch of Vikings. They named it the kraken. That's Norse, you know."

"The *kraken*?" exclaimed William, horrified. He'd seen pictures of it in a book at school – a gigantic squiddy thing with huge suckered tentacles wrapped around helpless sailors, squeezing them to death. No way could he deal with one of those.

Keep calm, he told himself. Remember what Odysseus said: despair is the enemy. "But it's going to sleep," he said, his voice coming out higher and squeakier than he'd have liked. "That's OK, isn't it? It won't be dangerous if it's asleep. Can't we just leave it alone?"

Zeus sighed deeply. "Unfortunately, it is when the kraken sleeps that it is at its most lethal."

William's shoulders drooped. "I suppose I should have guessed. Why's that, then?"

Zeus changed tack. "The world isn't quite as

well made as it should be—"

"I know that," interrupted William. "It's held together with string."

"Cosmic Grade Twine," corrected Zeus.

"Whatever."

"It was all such a rush job!" he complained. "I'm sorry to say that most of the continents were assembled very badly. The British Isles – and the rest of Europe for that matter – aren't as securely joined to the ocean floor as you might wish. Most of the land is simply balanced on the sea. It's anchored at one or two points to prevent it floating off, but I'm afraid Britain is about as stable as if it was perching on a pair of cocktail sticks. Safe enough, as long as nothing upsets its balance. But right now the sea monster is heading for a nice sleep right underneath it."

"What happens then?" asked William, dreading the answer.

"When the kraken sleeps, it snores," said Zeus. "And when it snores it sends up a stream of bubbles. Gigantic bubbles."

Zeus didn't say any more. He didn't need to. William knew exactly what the effect would be.

He turned and pressed the red button behind him. A jet of bubbles streaked to the surface. Zeus and William watched the plastic boat sink to the bottom of the glass tube.

"Oh, no," groaned William.

"Oh, yes." Zeus fixed his bright blue eyes on William's face. "When the kraken snores, the whole of Britain – the whole of Europe – will sink. Ever wondered why the planet's surface is two-thirds ocean? It didn't used to be, you know. Not at first. But the kraken would keep snuggling up under land masses for a little snooze. Have you heard of Atlantis?"

William nodded.

"It was a lovely place," sighed Zeus, "until the kraken got sleepy. It would be an awful shame to lose Europe to the same fate, don't you agree?"

ATHENE

William didn't have time to answer. At that moment something white shot across the museum and crashed into his stomach.

"Oooooof!" he gasped.

It was fortunate he was already sitting down, for the thing landed so hard that William was temporarily winded. He opened and closed his mouth like a goldfish, but all that came out was a faint croak.

"I told you to stay outside," Zeus said crossly.

William looked down. A very small owl was lying flat on its back in his lap, its grey eyes gazing up at him adoringly.

"Oh, but I couldn't," hooted the owl squeakily. "How could I stay out there knowing that *he* was in here?" The bird blinked rapidly, several times. It didn't have eyelashes, but if it had William had the distinct impression that they would have been fluttering hard.

Zeus sighed. "Meet my daughter," he said. "This is the goddess Athene."

"Thrilled to meet you at last," she gushed. "Gosh! You have exactly the same lovely hair. Copper! Fantastic!"

William thought he knew who she was talking about but wanted to make sure. "Same as who?" he asked.

"Odysseus," Athene sighed breathlessly. "My hero."

Zeus tutted and said to William, "She always did have a bit of a thing about him."

"Did not!" said the owl indignantly.

"Did too!" sniffed Zeus.

"Did not!" Athene squealed. "I just admired his manly courage, that's all. And his cleverness, his wit, his ingenuity and…"

Zeus said wearily, "See what I mean? There was no stopping her once she knew he had a living descendant. She insisted on tagging along. Terribly undignified! Really, Athene, it's most ungodlike to have a crush on a mortal."

"You're a fine one to talk!" she retorted. "Look who got stuck as a swan! All in pursuit of a pretty face."

Zeus pulled himself up to his full height. William sensed that the argument was about to get nasty. "Stop it!" he said firmly. Both gods looked at him. "Squabbling isn't going to help."

"He's right, you know," said Athene. She was doing the blinking thing again. "Wise, too. How marvellous!"

"Mmmm." William flushed and tried to change the subject. Picking Athene from his lap and setting her on the floor, he asked brightly, "So … how did you get stuck as an owl?"

"Oh, no! No, no, no!" She stretched her wings out. "I'm not stuck. Not at all. This is simply my travelling outfit." She gave William a twirl, rocking slowly from one taloned foot to another as she turned a full circle. "My human-shaped body is back at home." Athene blinked several times and said eagerly, "Would you like to see me in it?"

"For heaven's sake!" exploded Zeus. "There isn't time for this! We have a continent to save!" He turned to William. "Got any idea how to go about it?"

"Not really," said William honestly.

"I thought not." Zeus rubbed the place beneath his beak that would have been his chin with the tip of one wing. "We could do with some inspiration, not to mention assistance. You know, William, I think it's time I took you to Mount Olympus."

Zeus waddled purposefully across the museum floor and William followed. It was difficult to walk in a straight line because Athene was flapping in excited circles around his head.

At the bottom of the museum steps stood Pegasus, his coat so white that William was almost dazzled by the glare. When he saw William,

Pegasus whinnied in joyful greeting. His mane was shot through with streaks of silver and gold which rippled in the sunshine.

William couldn't stop himself. With rising excitement, he bounded down the steps two at a time, meaning to vault onto Pegasus in heroic fashion. Unfortunately, he was going so fast by the time he reached the bottom that he sailed clean over the horse's back and landed in an ungainly heap on the pavement.

The owl gave a girly giggle. "Oopsy-daisy!"

"Impressive," called Zeus. "Nice to see you haven't lost your touch." He plopped heavily down the steps. When he reached William he extended his bald wing stumps, pierced him with a look and said pointedly, "Aren't you forgetting something?"

William looked at Zeus, flightless as a penguin. He picked up the king of the gods and heaved him into position between Pegasus's wings. Then, performing a rather rusty, awkward vault, William mounted behind him.

The swan gave a loud belch and dribbled something warm and wet on William's head.

"Eeuw!" protested William. "I hope that's Lethe water."

"Of course it is. You don't think I'd deliberately be sick on you, do you?" The swan dribbled more water onto his own breast and then onto Pegasus's neck. It didn't make them invisible, but it meant that anyone who spotted them would instantly forget what they had seen.

"Aren't you going to splatter her?" William pointed at Athene, who was looping the loop

36

above the museum, impatient to be off.

"No," said Zeus. "She's old enough to take care of herself." He lifted his beak and called, "To Mount Olympus!"

Pegasus stretched his great wings. With one beat they took off, the air punching out with such force that it rocked the coach where William's classmates still sat, staring vacantly out of the windows. In two beats they reached the rooftops; in three, they were skimming over the houses of Brighton towards the Channel.

It took Athene a moment to realize they'd left. "Wait for me!" she squawked. It was the last thing she said for a long time. Pegasus flew so fast that she could only keep up with desperate, frantic flapping, and she was too out of breath to chat. William was relieved. He had the feeling that Athene's company might become a little wearing if he was exposed to it for too long.

In his excitement, William had forgotten quite how far it was from England to Greece. He started in high spirits because there was nothing as glorious as riding a flying horse: it made the rocket simulator seem dull in comparison. But after an hour he became uncomfortably aware of the bones in his bottom. After two hours, he felt as though they were trying to press their way out through his flesh. After three hours, the insides of his knees felt like they'd been rubbed hard with a sheet of sandpaper. And after four hours, his eyes were glazed and he was desperate for the journey to end. Pegasus could fly fast, but he wasn't as speedy as an aeroplane. It took several painful hours before Zeus announced, "We're here!", and Pegasus began his descent towards Mount Olympus.

William peered down curiously at the home of the gods. They sank through a layer of cold cloud but all he could see below him was a mountain top, as craggy and pointy and bleak as every other mountain he'd ever seen. He was stabbed with disappointment. He hadn't realized until that moment that he'd expected something more – a palace at the very least.

They hadn't even reached the bare peak when Pegasus stopped dead. William felt the thud of his hooves landing on something, but he couldn't see what. Calmly, the horse folded its wings. William looked below him nervously. There was nothing there. Pegasus was standing on air. Underneath his hooves was a dizzying drop of perhaps a thousand metres.

Zeus slid off sideways and landed on the emptiness with a loud *plap!*

"Come on, William, off you get."

"No way." He wasn't about to step into thin air, even if it was magically holding the swan up.

"What's got into you? Come down here at once."

"No," said William, twining his hands in the horse's mane just in case Zeus tried to force him to dismount.

"It's perfectly safe," chided Zeus.

"I'm staying here."

But just then the furiously flapping Athene crashed into the back of William's head and unbalanced him. He slid sideways: not much, but just enough for Zeus to reach up, grab his trouser leg in his beak and pull.

He was a remarkably strong bird. William resisted, screaming, "No! No! NO!!!", and hanging on to Pegasus's mane until the horse began snorting in pained protest. Not wanting to hurt him, William let go, grabbing at Zeus's neck instead: he was desperate to get hold of *something*.

He felt the *thwack* as he landed flat on his face but kept his eyes tight shut. From beneath his chest came an angry, muffled voice.

"Get off! Get off!! You're squashing me!"

William shifted a little to let Zeus pull his head free, but he kept hold of the swan's neck.

"You're strangling me," Zeus croaked. "Let go."

"Not until you get me on to something solid," said William through clenched teeth. "Don't leave me here."

"You are on something solid," snapped Zeus. "Look around you."

William opened his eyes and nearly threw up. Mountains stretched away into the distance on either side of him, the craggy rock sprouting from green wooded valleys far, far below. If he had been on an aeroplane, or even on the back of Pegasus, the view would have been spectacular. Spread-eagled in midair, with only a plucked swan to cling to, it was terrifying. A small, helpless gurgle escaped from William's throat.

He shut his eyes again. That was marginally better.

"Open them up," tutted Zeus irritably.

"No."

"Open them!"

"Don't want to."

"For the last time, William, OPEN YOUR EYES!"

Then William heard a voice – soft as silk, warm as summer sunshine, sweet as honey – dripping over him.

"Perhaps these will help," it said. William felt someone slip a pair of glasses onto his face.

He opened his eyes. Standing so close that the big toes almost touched his nose was a pair of feet.

William had never thought much about feet before. They were just there, on the ends of your legs. It had certainly never occurred to him that they could be beautiful.

These feet were gorgeous. William gazed help-lessly at them – bewitched by their loveliness – until Zeus's voice cut through the spell.

"Will you stop that, Aphrodite?" he snapped.

"But it's ages since I've entranced a mortal," came the whining reply.

"Switch it off."

"Can't I just allure him a little bit?"

"Switch it off now!"

"Please?" she begged.

"Do you really want me to throw a thunder-bolt?"

She sighed and tutted grumpily. And suddenly the feet were normal again. Uninteresting, slightly smelly, and in severe need of moisturizer. William stood up and looked at Zeus, bemused. He shook his head as if he was trying to get water out of his ears. "What was all that about?" he asked.

"Meet Aphrodite, goddess of love," Zeus intro-duced the woman who stood beside him. "She used to allure mortals all the time, but it's been aeons since she had the chance to use her powers of attraction. I didn't realize bringing you here would go to her head quite so much."

Released from Aphrodite's spell, William looked about him.

"WOW!" he exclaimed. With the spectacles on, he could suddenly see that he wasn't standing on nothingness. He was on a very solid floor consist-ing of extremely large paving slabs which stretched

42

away into the distance. But they weren't stone or marble. They seemed to be made of—

"Compressed clouds," said Zeus proudly. "Beautiful, aren't they?"

On either side of him, pillars the size of Nelson's Column formed an impressive avenue. William reached out a hand to prod the nearest one. It was warm to the touch and set his fingers tingling.

"What is this?" he asked.

"Solid sunlight," declared Zeus.

William stared upwards. Above him was a vaulted ceiling that rippled and blazed with red and purple and orange.

"And up there?" he pointed.

"Ah, yes," sighed Zeus. "Lovely, isn't it? That was my idea, you know. That's condensed sunset. Gorgeous, eh? I do have rather a flair for interior design."

"So why couldn't I see it before?"

"Yes, I'd forgotten about that. It was thoughtless of me, I do apologize. We had to introduce the Invisibility Programme a few hundred years ago," Zeus explained. "It wasn't a problem in the old days; no mortal would have been seen dead up here – they wouldn't have dared. But now, well, things are different. There are mountaineers crawling all over the place. And we can't have any old mortal wandering up and trying to steal our ambrosia."

"The glasses screen it out," whined the sulky Aphrodite. "My husband, Hephaestus, knocked them up for you. I would have thought I'd get a bit more gratitude."

William put his hand up to examine the glasses. They were enormous, and the lenses were made of hundreds of little glass hexagons all welded together. They felt – and probably looked – like the eyes of a bluebottle. "Thank you," said William sincerely.

Aphrodite beamed at him, sending William's heart soaring. Before he could throw himself at her feet, Zeus intervened.

"Don't start that again," he commanded. "Really, Aphrodite! If I'd known you'd be so daft, I'd never have brought him here." He turned to William. "Let's hope the others are a little more sensible."

"Others?"

"Yes, Mount Olympus seemed the best place to come. I thought we might need a little divine inter-vention to tackle the kraken."

An icy voice prickling with hostility interrupted him. "He might need it. But what on earth makes you think we will give it to him?"

William turned. He didn't know where they had come from – he hadn't heard anyone approach – but surrounding him were several figures, human-shaped, but not human-sized. They were

all so statuesque, so otherworldly, that he didn't
have to ask who had come out to meet him.

William could see at once that they were the
Olympic gods.

MOUNT OLYMPUS

"So this is our hero, is it?" A plump woman was looking William up and down with frosty disdain. "I must say I enjoyed watching him lying on the floor like that. Begging. Pleading. A very edifying little display. He's not what I'd call hero material. Why on earth should we waste our time helping him?"

"Who's she?" whispered William from the corner of his mouth.

"Hera," hissed Zeus in reply. "My dearly beloved wife."

Hera hadn't finished. "I don't know why you expect any of us to do anything anyway. So what if a few million mortals drown? Who cares if the British Isles sink?"

"Because, my dear," said Zeus grimly, "if the kraken settles under Britain, it'll affect the whole of Europe. The entire continent is unstable. Everything could go under. Including Greece. And I for one don't fancy being homeless."

Hera humphed, but said no more.

"I suppose I'd better introduce everyone," said Zeus to William. "And then we can start the meeting. This is Hera. Athene, you've already met. And Aphrodite, of course."

The lovely goddess fixed William with her limpid eyes and said breathily, "When you die, we can set you in the stars! So romantic!"

"Die?" said William, alarmed. "I'm not going to die, am I?"

"Not if I can help it," soothed Zeus. "Nice sentiment, Aphrodite, but hardly practical. The idea is for William to survive his mission."

"Oh." Aphrodite pouted, disappointed.

"This is Apollo," said Zeus, "and his sister Artemis."

"Hello," said William as his hand was clasped enthusiastically by the handsome god. William turned to smile at Artemis, but to his surprise she turned away sniffily before he could say anything.

"She doesn't much like men," explained Zeus. "Pay no attention." He walked over to a god who was hovering on winged sandals just above the tiled floor. "This is Hermes. And this," Zeus said, stopping in front of a god who appeared to be half man, half goat, "is Pan."

Pan opened his mouth in what William assumed was meant to be a welcoming smile but was more of a leer.

At the far end of the hall, a group of gods was huddled together, looking menacing.

"Who are they?" asked William nervously.

"Ah … yes… Well, I won't take you any closer to that lot, I think. Best to keep your distance. They're not what you'd call sociable. That's Ares, god of war, and his sister, Eris, goddess of discord."

"And who are all the others?"

"Their followers. That's Pain, and that wobbly one over there is Panic. The skinny creature is Famine, obviously. That black blobby thing is Oblivion and those are his sons, Fear and Terror. Not the most pleasant family."

William's spine prickled as he looked at the grim assortment of deities.

"That's pretty much everyone," concluded Zeus. "Hades isn't here yet, but I think he'll be along later. Now, everyone," he addressed the gods, "I've brought William here to gather some inspiration. Does anyone have any ideas?"

There was a deafening silence as all the gods seemed to develop a sudden fascination with the floor tiles.

It was broken at last by Athene hopping up and down and squawking, "Oh! Oh! I know! I know! He could petrify it. That would be marvellous!"

"I don't have to face another Gorgon, do I?" William was trying to be heroic, but the thought of tackling both a Gorgon and a sea monster was enough to make his knees wobble.

Zeus shook his head. "No, your plan wouldn't work, Athene. We're out of Gorgons. William here turned the last two to stone."

There were muttered sighs and heavy tutting from some of the gods, and William found himself mumbling, "Sorry."

"Can't be helped," said Zeus briskly. "You weren't to know the kraken was going to get sleepy."

Apollo's hand shot up in the air. "He could fight it, like Heracles. Leap down its throat fully armed and chop it to bits from inside!"

Zeus gave a proud chuckle. "Ah, yes, Heracles! What a fighter! He was one of my offspring, William."

"The whole of Greece was once peppered with your offspring," grumbled Hera. "You should be ashamed of yourself."

She threw a look of such bitter resentment at William that he couldn't help whispering to Zeus, "Was Odysseus a son of yours too?"

"No, no. Odysseus was mortal through and through, same as you. So I'm afraid you can't tackle the kraken with brute force – you're far too weak for that."

"Thanks," said William.

"Now, don't be offended, William, you know it's true. It takes a splash of divine blood to give any-one the strength to fight a monster. I don't know … perhaps this was all a wasted journey. This lot are useless at anything but quarrelling."

The gods erupted into a loud, argumentative protest at this remark. It sounded like a cosmic ver-sion of wet playtime. Zeus heaved a deep sigh.

"See what I mean?"

William didn't answer. Suddenly all the hairs on the back of his neck had stood up. A chill swept through his body and his arms pimpled with goose flesh. He shivered, teeth clacking noisily together. Looking around for the source of the icy draught, William noticed ink-black tendrils creeping over the cloud tiles towards him. Writhing around his ankles, snakes of pitch-blackness twisted and started to curl up his legs.

Stifling a scream, William turned to Zeus, but

the king of the gods wasn't looking at him. His bright blue eyes were fixed on a new arrival, and he was grumbling, "About time too!"

Entering the hall, wreathed in a cape of night, was a gigantic figure from whom the tendrils were emanating. William hoped desperately that whoever it was wasn't going to lower his hood. He didn't want to know what lay beneath it.

"Who's that?" squeaked William.

"My brother Hades," replied Zeus, "Lord of the Underworld, king of the dead."

William's hair had gone strangely stiff and heavy, and he realized that icicles were hanging down like a spiky fringe across his forehead. By now, his teeth were chattering so loudly that Zeus at last turned to look at him.

"You can switch off the Spectral Chill, Hades," said Zeus wearily. "We're not impressed. We've seen it a million times before."

"He hasn't," said a cold voice. The ghostly figure was pointing at William.

"I didn't bring him here to be terrorized. We're supposed to be helping him, not scaring him witless. Stop showing off."

With a sigh of disappointment, Hades threw back his hood and William's hair bounced back into its usual tight curls.

Without the hood, Hades looked reassuringly normal. He was in fact smaller than the other gods and slightly paler – a result, William supposed, of spending so much time in the weird nothingness of the Underworld.

Hades peeled off his cloak and stepped aside to reveal who was standing behind him. "I've brought you a visitor," he announced. "I've let him out on day release. Thought he might be able to help."

"Oh, good god!" cried Zeus with enthusiasm. "Clever thinking, Hades."

William looked and was delighted to see the familiar figure of Odysseus crossing the palace floor to meet him. He caught a glimpse of Athene fainting in a feathery heap before his ancestor enfolded him in a manly hug. Or at least tried to. The last time Odysseus had done this, William's face had sunk into his chest and he'd got an unnerving sight of all his internal organs. This time the reverse happened: Odysseus embraced him with such gusto that he passed straight through William's body and emerged, slightly surprised, behind him.

"Mount Olympus!" he exclaimed, giving his head a good shake as if he'd got little bits of William stuck in his ears. "The world is full of marvels!" He turned and grinned broadly. "It is good to see you once more, descendant of mine. How goes your next adventure?"

"Erm ... not very well at the moment," William confessed.

"What challenge do you face?"

"I've got to sort out a sea monster."

"A sea monster! A mighty task indeed." Odysseus rubbed his spectral hands together while he considered the matter. "How do you intend to combat the beast?" he asked.

"Well," said William, "it looks like I can't fight it or petrify it, so I'm not sure what to do… I'm a bit short of inspiration."

Odysseus paced briskly up and down but seemed as lacking in ideas as William. He said nothing for a long time and at last muttered, "The creature must be slain somehow. Else it shall crush the shipping and devour the populace."

"Well, yes, I think it will do that too," explained William. "But that's not why I've got to do something about it. The real problem is that it's going to go to sleep…"

As the words left his mouth, William felt something stir in the dark recesses of his brain. The seed of an idea was beginning to sprout.

Sleep. The image of his mum's pink hair on the pillow swam into his mind. Her hand, swivelling like a raised periscope. He couldn't turn the kraken to stone, and he wasn't strong enough to fight it. But maybe – just maybe – it didn't need to be killed. Perhaps the answer was something completely different...

Suddenly, William knew exactly what was needed.

"Zeus!" said William. "We need to get to Spitflos!"

HEPHAESTUS

"Spitflos?" asked Zeus. "Why Spitflos?"

"Coffee!" exclaimed William. "My dad makes the strongest coffee ever, according to my mum. We need him to make up a whole bucketload of it. If we can get the kraken to drink that, it will wake up! And if it wakes up, nothing will sink, will it?"

"An ingenious plan!" cried Odysseus. "I know not this drink of which you speak, but by all the gods I like the sharpness of your mind!"

"Yes…" Zeus was a little less enthusiastic. "It does have a few flaws, unfortunately."

"Flaws?" William asked. "What flaws?"

"For a start," Zeus said, "how do you intend to transport the liquid, William? A bucket of coffee will simply wash away in the sea."

"OK, then, it'll have to go in something with a lid, won't it? Easy."

"Even supposing we can find something with a lid, how can we get it into the creature's mouth?"

"Don't know. Haven't you got anything up here that we can use?"

"Regrettably, no," answered Zeus. "Immortals don't have much use for such things—"

"Ask Hephaestus," interrupted Aphrodite. "He can make anything."

"Good thinking," said Zeus. "Perhaps your idea has potential, William. Let's go and see Hephaestus. He'll be in his forge."

Leaving Odysseus to the twittering Athene, William followed Zeus down several corridors, the king of the gods pointing out each change of colour scheme as they went.

"That's the dining hall. Took my inspiration from a Greek salad, you see. Walls of cucumber green, floor of tomato red, feta-cheese-white columns, with a ceiling as black as olives. Nice, don't you think?"

"Mmmm," agreed William. But his mind wasn't really on interior design. He was too busy wondering how he could persuade a sea monster to drink coffee and whether he'd be eaten alive in the process.

They heard Hephaestus long before they saw him. The clanging sound of metal pounding on metal echoed down the corridor, so loud that William's teeth rattled. And then he felt the raging heat and heard the crackle of roaring flames.

William knew he was about to enter a forge, but even so, the sight set his eyes popping with aston-ishment.

The room was vast. On the far side, a god that William took to be Hephaestus was beating some-thing over his anvil with a giant hammer. From the ceiling hung his creations: a net of gold, so finely wrought that its threads were almost invisible; a lance with an end so sharp that the air around it rippled strangely as if it had been cut to ribbons. A winged helmet took flight as they entered, flapping nervously across the forge and perching on a hook near Hephaestus.

William looked for the source of the heat. Instead of the furnace he expected, he saw a ring of rock that protruded up through the tiled floor like a

boiled egg with the top sliced off. At its centre, where the yolk would be, were not burning coals but a liquid, molten fire. The heat was so strong that William's skin tightened over his cheekbones and his nose began peeling. He started sweating – he could feel moisture trying to squeeze itself out of his pores – but it dried before it had even reached the surface. William was shocked to realize that he was looking at lava. Hephaestus's furnace was the bowl of an active volcano. As he watched, the god took a pair of bellows and puffed air at it. Lava and flames shot towards the ceiling.

"Wow!" William gasped, and the god turned.

When he saw them, Hephaestus lowered his bellows and lurched towards them, limping heavily. Noticing William's scalded face and Zeus's rapidly blistering skin, he steered them behind an elaborately crafted screen to protect them from the heat. He stood no taller than William, and his back was curled as if he'd spent so long hunched over his anvil that he couldn't now straighten up.

"We need your help," began Zeus.

Hephaestus nodded. "Tell me what you require." His voice was a throaty rasp as if his vocal cords had long ago been dried out by the searing flames of his forge. Talking sounded painful, and he didn't waste any more words but stood staring at William waiting for him to explain.

"I want to put a whole load of coffee – that's a sort of drink – in a container so it won't get washed away in the sea. And I need to get it down a monster's throat so maybe I could have some sort of tube to squirt it in with?"

Hephaestus didn't say anything but frowned, considering the request. William's eyes fell on the bellows in the god's hand.

"Those might do!" exclaimed William.

"These?" Hephaestus held them up.

"Yes! They'd be perfect." William looked at the bellows more closely and realized that part of them was made of leather. He rubbed a hand over it. "Oh," he said, disappointed. "That's not waterproof, is it?"

"No," agreed Hephaestus gruffly, "but—"

Zeus interrupted, "His skill is astonishing. He can spin gold so fine that no one – neither mortal nor god – can see it. He's made shields that shine as bright as a mirror. Sandals which render the wearer invisible. He can make waterproof bellows, William. Don't doubt it." He turned to Hephaestus. "How long?" he asked.

"One hour," was the curt reply. He didn't say any more but turned and limped back to his anvil. The beating began again.

"Thank you!" William called after him, but Hephaestus didn't even wave his hammer in reply.

They left the forge and started to walk back along the corridors through the interconnecting courtyards and halls of the palace.

"There is another problem," said Zeus. "How in the world are we going to stay underwater long enough to find the beast?"

"Underwater?" said William, horrified. "Why do we have to go underwater? Can't we tempt it up to the surface?"

"How?"

"I don't know. With a boat or something. Didn't you say it snacks on ships?"

"Sometimes," replied Zeus dully. "But it's not hungry when it's this sleepy. No, we'll need to get beneath the waves. How long can you hold your breath, William?"

"I can do a length underwater," said William thoughtfully. "But that's not going to be enough, is it? I suppose we could get hold of some scuba diving stuff." William didn't feel confident about this idea. He wouldn't know what to do with a tank of oxygen even if he knew where to find one, and he was pretty sure you needed to be trained. In any case, how could he fit a mask to a swan?

They walked along in depressed silence, Zeus's webbed feet slapping noisily on the compressed cloud slabs.

And then suddenly Hera was standing before them, a broad smile pasted across her face.

"Hello, boys," she crooned softly. "I couldn't help overhearing. Need to get underwater, do you? Let me help. I have the very things."

She raised an eyebrow and smiled. It was the most chilling spectacle William had seen since he'd arrived on Mount Olympus.

SPITFLOS

Hera wouldn't tell them what she had planned. All she would say (with a broad wink at the man-hating Artemis) was that she'd bring her mysterious items to Spitflos.

"As soon as Hephaestus has finished your little contraption, you get yourselves off. Fill it up with coffee and I'll meet you on the beach afterwards. I've got the perfect solution, I promise." She pierced William with a steely stare and gave another terrifying smile. "Trust me."

William thought he'd rather trust a Minotaur but he seemed to have very little choice. He couldn't think of a way of surviving underwater, and Hera had offered to help. She was a goddess, wasn't she? She was bound to have access to more stuff than he could summon up. He just couldn't imagine what, that was the problem. And he didn't like the looks and sniggers that passed between Hera and Artemis. It was like they were making fun of him. Or Zeus. It made William squirm.

Hephaestus, at least, was straightforward. Exactly one hour after Zeus and William had left his forge, the god limped into the hall with an enormous pair of bellows. The spout part was as long as William's arm and was capped with a silver screw top. The handles were of sturdy steel – strong, yet light enough for William to carry without too much difficulty. The bellows were of a strange golden alloy, so thinly beaten that they folded like supple leather, but so strong that even the sharpest knife couldn't cut them. Hephaestus had attached a metal rod that would pull down and brace the bellows open when they were full of liquid, so that William wouldn't accidentally squirt the coffee out before he was ready. And he'd also thoughtfully fixed a pair of slender straps to the sides so that William could put the entire thing on his back, like an oddly shaped rucksack.

Without further delay, they set off for Spitflos.

Bidding a fond farewell to Odysseus, William hoisted Zeus onto Pegasus but found he couldn't quite manage a vault with the golden bellows on his back. He had to suffer the indignity of being picked up by Hera and put astride as if he were a toddler on a rocking horse.

He hadn't realized until Pegasus soared away from the palace that it was already dark.

When they landed on Spitflos it was so late that everything on the island was closed, including his father's taverna.

William was worn out, but there was no chance of getting a good night's sleep in a comfortable bed. The beach would just have to do. Unloading the bellows from his back, he sat down. The sand still held a little of the day's warmth, so he wriggled around, digging himself down into it like an oversized lugworm. Shutting his eyes, he drifted off to sleep.

The sand that had seemed so soft to begin with

got harder and colder as the night progressed. By the time the sun started to rise, William felt as if he was embedded in concrete. Bleary-eyed and aching in all sorts of places, he sat up and yawned. Looking about him he realized with a jolt that Pegasus was nowhere to be seen.

"He's gone!" William shook the pimply swan beside him until he woke up.

"Well, of course he's gone," answered Zeus irritably. "He wouldn't want to hang about and get spotted. He'll come when I call him, don't worry."

Shaking sand from his ears and picking a shell off his cheek, William heaved the bellows onto his aching shoulders. Then, with Athene flapping along behind them, he and Zeus made their way from the beach towards the taverna that was owned by Nikos Popidopolis, William's father. It was so early that no one else was up, and William's footsteps were unnaturally loud on the dusty road. Zeus's webbed feet sounded like a diver fleeing the clutches of the sea.

Early as it was, Nikos was already opening up. The smell of coffee reached William's nostrils long before he entered the taverna.

"That's the stuff," he whispered.

"Are you sure?" asked Zeus. "Smells vile."

"Yes," replied William. "A bellyful of that will wake the kraken, no problem."

In the taverna, Nikos stood behind the counter, revving up the espresso machine like a racing driver waiting for the flag to drop.

William coughed, and with the smoothly charming smile of a professional host, Nikos turned to face him.

"You my first customer! You up early. You want breakfast?" he said. Then he saw who it was, and his smile fell off and smashed into fragments on the floor.

"William?" he asked uncertainly. "What you do here, eh? I no expect you."

"No…" said William. He hadn't thought about what he might say to his father. His mind had been fixed entirely on the coffee and the kraken: he didn't have a suitable explanation for his sudden appearance.

Fortunately, Nikos didn't seem to notice immediately. He was staring over William's shoulder nervously. "Where your mother? She here too?"

"No. I'm all alone."

"Phew!" Nikos relaxed for a moment, but then his brow furrowed into an anxious frown. "Alone? You come all this way alone? You no run away? You no in trouble?"

"Not exactly…" faltered William. "It's a bit of a long story."

"Long story, eh? Tell you what. You have breakfast first. Then you tell it to your father, OK?"

William nodded, and without another word Nikos handed him a glass of freshly squeezed orange juice and a bowl of creamy yoghurt drizzled with honey. After a night on the cold, hard sand it tasted as good as ambrosia.

Pouring himself his first coffee of the day, Nikos came round the counter to perch on a bar stool and listen to William's explanation. It was only then that he noticed the bald, sunburnt swan and the small white owl at William's feet.

"Eeuw!" he said, revolted. "Go 'way! Shoo! Shoo! Get outta here, you dirty birds."

Looking mortally offended, Zeus complied, waddling out of the taverna and onto the dusty street. With a screech of protest, Athene flapped through the open door and perched in a nearby olive tree.

While Nikos's back was turned, William unscrewed the phial of Lethe water Zeus had thoughtfully provided and poured a drop into his father's coffee. Once he'd drunk it, the problem of what to tell Nikos would fade away, along with his father's memory. Meanwhile, William had to think of something fast. It was strange enough him being here at all, especially without his mother. But popping over for a bucket of coffee to wake the kraken wasn't the kind of explanation that grown-ups liked to hear.

Nikos came back and sat himself down beside

his son, staring suspiciously at the golden bellows. He made no attempt to drink his coffee but just stared expectantly, waiting to hear the story.

William scraped his bowl clean. He licked the spoon until every trace of honey was gone. Then he finished his juice. Slowly – draining every last drop from the glass and sticking a finger in to scrape off the orangey bits clinging to the sides.

"Can I have some more?" he asked, hopefully.

"Story first. Food later."

"Your coffee's getting cold," said William.

Nikos grunted. He reached out and took his cup in the palm of one hand. He didn't lift it to his lips but sat, head on one side, waiting for his son to begin.

William racked his brains but couldn't come up with anything. He was no good at lying. The truth was just going to have to do.

"It's like this," he began. "It was yesterday. It started normally enough. I had a school trip, you see."

Nikos swirled the coffee in his cup. He still didn't drink it.

"We went to the museum…" said William slowly.

Nikos lifted the cup to his lips, eyeing William over the brim with raised brows.

"Then... Well... It was a bit of a surprise, really. Zeus arrived."

It was the wrong thing to say. Nikos coughed, spluttering a mouthful of coffee over William's school shirt. He laughed drily. "Is a good joke," he said. And then, sternly, "Now you tell me what happened or I ring your mother. You have an argument with her?"

William seized on the suggestion. "Yes," he mumbled, hanging his head pitifully.

Nikos nodded understandingly. "She a hard woman to live with sometime," he commiserated. "What you two argue about, eh?"

William didn't have to answer. The very thought of Kate in a temper was enough to make Nikos drain his cup in one go. His mind cleared. William could see it happening. Nikos's eyes glazed for a moment. When they refocused, he was looking at William as if he'd never seen him before. The professional smile was switched on, as bright as a light bulb.

"You my first customer! You up early! You want

breakfast?" Nikos slid back behind the counter, eager to serve a tourist.

"Yes, please," said William brightly. "I'd like a coffee. The stronger the better."

When it was placed before him, William took it and dived below the counter. Removing the bellows from his back, he unscrewed the lid and poured the coffee carefully down the nozzle. It was going to take an awful lot of cups to fill it, he thought anxiously. Fortunately, Nikos didn't notice.

It was like being on a repeating film loop. William bobbed back up, Nikos turned, saw him – as if for the first time – and asked what he wanted. The answer was always the same.

"Coffee, please. The stronger the better."

After one hundred and eighty-seven cups, the espresso machine was steaming ferociously as if it were about to explode. And poor Nikos was reeling queasily, dizzy from turning around and around from the bar to the coffee machine.

By now the sun was higher and there was movement in the streets outside. The locals were up and about, and it wouldn't be long before the hotel guests started coming in for their breakfast. The bellows weren't quite full, but William couldn't wait any longer. He heaved the contraption onto his back. It was heavy now, and if he leant too far to one side, he could feel the weight of liquid threatening to unbalance him completely. With a wave to his vague and dizzy father, he staggered to join Zeus on the street.

Slooshing gently, they made their way back to the beach. It was empty, although some holiday-makers had already laid out their towels on sun loungers to reserve them.

"Don't know why they don't just piddle on the things," grumbled Zeus, "like dogs do. Would be a whole lot simpler."

Zeus threw his head back, and William stuffed his fingers in his ears. He knew from experience that Zeus was about to emit an ear-piercing squawk to call Pegasus.

But before he could let out a sound, Hera and Artemis appeared, fluttering across the sand towards them on two pairs of weary-looking winged sandals. And stuffed under their arms appeared to be the sagging bodies of two dead mermaids.

SEA NYMPHS

They weren't mermaids. Hera was very definite about that. They were sea nymphs, she informed William, and they most certainly weren't dead. Neither were they bodies: not in the sense that William had first thought. They were more like costumes that Hera was loaning from her wardrobe for the occasion.

"I wasn't aware you had these," said Zeus, his eyes narrowing with suspicion.

"Being divine doesn't mean you know everything," replied Hera. "You're not the only one who can travel in disguise."

Sensing another almighty squabble brewing, William intervened. "What are they for?" he asked brightly.

"You need to get underwater, don't you?" Hera fixed William with a stare that could have iced over the Mediterranean. "Sea nymphs have a vast lung capacity. Not to mention the tail strength of a whale. You can dive as deep as you like for as long as you like once you're inside this."

"Are you absolutely sure of that?" asked Zeus.

Hera glared. "Well … more or less. I'm not saying it's *impossible* to drown. You'll need to come up for air from time to time. But what alternative do you have?"

Zeus stared at the limp nymphs lying on the sand. He looked back at Hera.

"A simple 'thank you' will suffice," said Hera sniffily.

"Thank you," said Zeus reluctantly. He turned to

William. "I'll take the bigger one, shall I?"

William couldn't answer. He was overcome with hot, squirming embarrassment but couldn't find the right words to protest. Before he could manage a single syllable, Zeus changed from one body to another.

When William was very small he'd had a rubber ring with a curving swan's head at the front. It had been punctured when he'd bounced on it, and he remembered the way its head had listed sadly sideways and then drooped onto a plastic wing. Now, before his eyes, the plucked, pimpled form of Zeus deflated until it lay on the beach drained of air, of vibrancy, of life. Beside it the sea nymph inflated, puffing up to massive proportions and then energetically flicking a long, powerful tail.

She was a vastly buxom thing, shapely and statuesque as a ship's figurehead with splendid hair that Zeus began patting fussily.

"I do hope this will survive the journey," he fretted. "I'd hate to end up looking a frightful mess."

"Zeus?" said William uncertainly.

"Yes?" The nymph looked at William with startling blue eyes. It was odd seeing those eyes in that body, but there was no doubt they belonged to the king of the gods. "Come along, William, there's no time to waste."

"No!" protested William. "I'm not changing into that."

"Why ever not?"

William flushed scarlet. "It's a girl!" he hissed.

"Of course it's a girl! Whoever heard of a male nymph?"

"I won't," said William, folding his arms across his chest and sticking his chin stubbornly in the air. The body might be perfect for the job, but there were limits to how far a hero should go to save the world and William felt he'd reached his. He wasn't dressing up as a girl for anyone.

But it seemed he didn't have much choice in the matter. One moment he was standing squarely on the sand looking stern, chin jutting out, eyes squinting in fury, and the next, he was being squeezed out of his own body. It was revolting. Like toothpaste being squirted from a tube. Like Coke being slurped up a straw. He was being squashed and squidged, compressed and forced out through his right nostril like a very long, very sticky length of string.

"STOP IT!" yelled William. "NO!!!" But try as he might, he made no sound: he had no voice. He'd left it behind in his nice, familiar William-shaped body. For a second or two he was floating loose and free in the warm air, invisible as the scent of orange blossom, then *bang!* He was a sea nymph. A sea nymph with... He could hardly bear to look down at what was on his chest. It was discreetly covered by a shell bikini top but it didn't feel a very secure garment to William. He flushed as pink as it was possible to flush and immediately turned to his own sadly deflated form. Without a word, he tugged off his coffee-stained school shirt and buttoned it firmly over the shells.

William was mortified about his new shape, but Zeus was full of enthusiasm.

"How can you be happy about this?" said William reproachfully. "It's so humiliating."

"Frankly, William," answered Zeus crisply, tucking a stray wisp of hair behind his ear, "anything's a welcome change from the swan. I've been stuck inside that teeny-tiny thing for centuries. It's a little cramped, you know. And it's not like I can even fly until my feathers grow back, can I?" Flicking his

tail with relish, Zeus showered the nearby sun loungers with sand. "No," he said, "I have a feeling I'm going to enjoy this."

Hera was less than careful as she picked up the deflated swan's body. Clutching it by one foot she slung it carelessly over her arm, letting its head bang hard on the sand as she glided away, winged sandals flapping furiously under her weight. William watched Artemis roll up his body like a sleeping bag and tuck it under her arm.

"What are you going to do with that?" he asked plaintively.

"There's a cave over there, see?" She pointed to a small hole at the foot of a rocky outcrop. "I'll tuck it in there. It will be perfectly safe until you return." She gave William a chilly little smile. Then she added, "*If* you return, that is. I don't think anyone's met the kraken before and lived to tell the tale."

"That's enough, Artemis," growled Zeus. "Don't alarm the boy."

The goddess turned and left but not before saying in a voice heavy with menace, "I do hope you don't meet Poseidon."

But before William could ask her why, she was off again, gliding serenely across the sand.

The sound of tourists approaching the beach stirred Zeus into action and he began flopping like an elephant seal towards the turquoise water. Strapping the bellows onto his back, William followed, lolloping awkwardly across the sand. He reached the waves just as the first sun-worshippers set foot on the beach, and swam away to the sounds of tourists shaking out their towels and angrily wiping heaps of sand from their sun loungers.

INKY DEPTHS

The bellows that had sloshed around and been so cumbersome on dry land became weightless once they were in the sea. William had always thought he was a good swimmer, but having a tail was a completely new experience. With one flick he was gliding through the water with sinuous ease, his golden locks streaming out behind him like ribbons in the wind. He followed Zeus around the headland, away from the prying eyes of tourists, and when they reached a secluded bay, William couldn't help himself – he dived deep into the cool, indigo depths. He'd been snorkelling before, but this was a whole new world. He didn't need a mask or a breathing tube; he wasn't floating on top, watching it as an observer; he was part of the ocean. It was exhilarating, intoxicating – even if he did have the body of a girl – and for a moment William was quite delirious with excitement. Above him, he saw Zeus making frantic signals, one finger to his lips, the other hand beckoning William to come back.

He would. But he was going to do it in style. With several beats of his powerful tail, William shot like a bullet towards the sunlight, breaching the surface into the warm air, like a dolphin, before re-entering the water so smoothly there was hardly a ripple. He laughed aloud in sheer delight, but Zeus was frowning crossly.

"WILL … YOU … STOP … THAT," he said between gritted teeth. "There are one or two things I need to warn you about."

"Oh," said William flatly. He had a feeling he wasn't going to like this. Zeus's voice sounded just like it had when he'd first told William about the Gorgons. Whatever was coming wasn't going to be nice. "Go on, then," he sighed.

They were bobbing in the waves, their heads just above the water. Athene came in to land, perching on Zeus's flowing locks so she could join the conversation.

"We need to be very, very careful," said Zeus quietly. "We're in Poseidon's realm now. I have no power here."

"But he's your brother, isn't he?"

"Indeed he is. But we're not what you might call close."

William had seen enough of the gods squabbling to understand what he meant. "He wouldn't hurt us, though, would he?"

"He won't hurt me. I am family, after all. But you're a different matter."

The thought of the sea god disliking him personally was a new and uncomfortable one for William. "Why?" he asked nervously.

"Poseidon was never exactly fond of Odysseus."

"He hated him," said Athene eagerly. "Loathed and detested him. Wanted to wipe him from the face of the earth!"

"He never forgave Odysseus for blinding the Cyclops, I'm afraid – the one-eyed monster was one of his offspring. Quite understandable, I suppose."

"But that was nothing to do with me," protested William.

"No, well, immortals have awfully long memories. You're Odysseus's descendant. That'll be enough for Poseidon."

"If he finds you, you're done for," said Athene helpfully.

"*If* he finds you," repeated Zeus. "But we're not going to let him, are we?"

"Certainly not," said Athene stoutly, fluffing out her feathers.

"Now, William," continued Zeus, "the best way of going about all this is by being discreet. The real sea nymphs stick to the deep ocean these days, so with luck we shouldn't run into any of them. If we keep to the shoreline and proceed with caution we should avoid detection altogether. So no more acrobatics, please."

"OK," agreed William.

"It was terribly good, though," gushed Athene. "I was impressed. You make a lovely sea nymph."

"Thank you," said William. He wasn't at all sure he liked the compliment.

* * *

Proceeding with caution wasn't easy. The shore-line of each island was crammed with swimmers and snorkellers. Further out, there were wind-surfers and scuba divers and people bombing about on jet skis. There were plenty of fishermen too, whose lines and nets were a constant hazard.

Athene flew ahead, wheeling back to warn them every time she spotted a boat, and then they'd dive deep and cruise above the sea bed.

Geography wasn't William's strong point, but he knew that swimming around the coast to Britain would take much longer than flying overland on Pegasus. Did they have enough time? His mind was making calculations as they knifed through the water, coming up for the occasional breath of air like a pair of porpoises. Today was Tuesday. The kraken was due to arrive in the English Channel on Friday. If they kept this pace up, they should just about manage it.

But then everything changed.

William heard something. The faintest noise. Far away. Deep down. An exquisite sound – so beauti-ful that he wasn't sure if it was even music. It was like nothing he'd ever heard before. He stopped swimming and hung motionless in the water, his golden hair billowing around his face, obscuring his vision. There was silence. He couldn't hear a thing but the sound of Zeus's tail beating as he swam further and further ahead. William made no attempt to follow. Instead he turned, slowly revolving, trying to catch the direction from which the sound had come.

Silence. Stillness. But then the current whirled, and there it was again – carried on the water like a faint strain of music on a gust of wind. The slightest trace of a yearning melody pierced William's chest and hooked him under the ribs as fast as a caught fish. Everything – the kraken, the British Isles, the millions of people who would drown – vanished from his mind. All he could think about was finding its source. He had to hear more of it. Nothing else mattered.

He swam slowly, ears craving the haunting music. It drew him down, growing no louder but becoming more persistent as the sea thickened and darkened all about him.

William only stopped when he could swim no

deeper. He was on the ocean floor, in the middle of a circle of statues. Little light penetrated there, but with his sea nymph's eyes, he could just make out the shapes of winged figures. He thought they might be women, but their faces were blurred, worn away by time and the movement of the constantly churning currents. Even at the heart of the circle, the music was barely audible. It was the ghost of a song; the echo of a melody so beautiful that William lay, enraptured, on the sandy sea bed, his whole being hungry for the next delicious phrase.

He sighed, barely aware of the stream of bubbles that rose from his mouth. He hardly felt the pain of his lungs aching for oxygen; the immense weight of water crushing his ribs; his heartbeat becoming faint and erratic. He shut his eyes to better hear the elusive notes that drifted from statue to statue.

By the time he was seized around the waist and yanked upwards, William was almost comatose. Even so, he still tried to fight against whatever it was that was dragging him away from the bewitching songs of the ancient stones. But he was

weak now, too weak to resist the hands that held him, the tail that thrashed furiously against the water and propelled him towards the light. Only when his head broke the surface, and his lungs drew in a desperate gasp of air, was the spell broken. In the sunshine, he could hear nothing.

Huffing and puffing, dizzy from the lack of oxygen, William looked about him in confusion. Athene was flying anxiously above the waves, fluttering in tense little circles around his head. Holding him up – towing him towards a secluded little beach and heaving him onto the sand – was Zeus.

For a long time they sat half in and half out of the water, William easing the bellows' weight by leaning against a rock. Zeus and Athene waited for him to recover, but by the time he felt normal again, the sun had begun to sink into the sea.

"What was that music?" asked William.

"Sirens," sighed Zeus. "I'd forgotten about them. They used to bewitch sailors with their songs and lure them to their deaths on the rocks. They were turned to stone long ago by Jason and his Argonauts. They sank to the bottom, but their power hasn't entirely gone. That was a very near miss."

"Crikey," said William. All of a sudden the darkening waters of the Mediterranean seemed a less than friendly place to be. "Is there anything else I should worry about?"

"Apart from the kraken?"

William nodded.

"Unfortunately, yes," answered Zeus. "First thing in the morning, we'll cross over to the coast of Italy. Then we have to get past Scylla and Charybdis."

"Who are they?" William asked, knowing full well he wasn't going to like the answer.

"Charybdis is a whirlpool, and Scylla's a multi-headed man-eating monster," replied Zeus. "Good night, William. Sleep well."

SCYLLA AND CHARYBDIS

They set off at first light, just as the sky was turning from a rich velvety blue to a rather less appealing steely grey. Crossing from Greece to Italy meant a rapid dash across the deep waters of the Adriatic. Zeus would have preferred to have stuck closer to the shore, but going up the coast of Croatia and back down the length of Italy would take too long. They needed to reach the English Channel by the quickest route possible. They would have to risk it.

It was a short but uncomfortable crossing. William was aware of things lurking in the depths. He felt eyes watching him, though whether they were those of suspicious sea nymphs or anxious fish there was no way of knowing.

They reached the heel of Italy's boot as the sky changed from grey to pink and then blue. They didn't pause for breakfast. William discovered a passion for raw sardines, snatching handfuls from each silvery shoal they swam through, swallowing them whole and finding to his surprise that he relished the wriggling sensation as they went down.

As they sped along the sole of Italy's boot, Zeus filled William in on Scylla and Charybdis.

"They're right on the toe of the boot, so to speak. You know where Sicily is?"

"No," confessed William.

"It's the island that looks like a football. You know, as if the boot of Italy's going to kick it."

William squinted in concentration as he tried hard to remember a map of Italy. Or of anywhere for that matter. He couldn't really picture it.

Zeus gave up.

"It hardly matters," he said. "The point is we have to go through a narrow channel between Italy and Sicily. And that's where Scylla and Charybdis are."

"Can't we go another way?"

"Unfortunately not. If we cut round Sicily we'd

be shredded by the rocks. They move around on the sea bed, you know, crushing anyone or anything that goes too near. Terribly dangerous. And I don't want to go into the really deep water because of Poseidon. No, we're going to have to do the Strait of Messina. As long as we keep to one side, far away from the whirlpool of Charybdis, we should be fine."

"And Scylla?"

Zeus didn't quite meet his eyes. "Well ... I don't think she gets out much these days. She's probably retired. Besides, we're nymphs, not sailors. I'm sure she won't be interested in us." Zeus sounded confident, but William noticed he was chewing his lip.

Athene didn't help. Each time William surfaced, she squawked bits of information at him – things he could have done without knowing.

"Odysseus managed to get through," she said.

"Did he? Oh, good." William dived.

"Mind you, he lost a few sailors," she added as he resurfaced.

"How?"

"Scylla ate them."

"What?!"

"She's a lot older now than she was then," soothed Zeus. "Even monsters age, William. We'll be safe. She'll probably be fast asleep, and if she isn't ... well, her teeth must be quite worn down by now. They'll be blunt. Harmless. You'll see."

Zeus was wrong. Scylla's teeth were neither blunt nor harmless.

When they approached the narrow strait, the monster was fast asleep in a cave near the top of the sheer cliff face which loomed high above the sea. If William hadn't been quite so surprised by the whirlpool, she would have remained there, snoring softly, and they might have passed her by without incident. Unfortunately, William decided to dive as deep as he could to avoid Scylla and instead came eyeball to eyeball with the most hideous creature he'd ever seen.

She was squatting on the sea bed, spindly legs stretched out before her like a pair of matchsticks, quite unable to support the weight of her vast belly. Her head was thrown back, her cavernous mouth open wide and sucking in water as though

she had a thirst that could never be quenched. She made no effort to harm William, raising a limp hand and waving it weakly at him as if in greeting. But she didn't turn her head, didn't stop drinking in the whirling sea water that was inflating her body like a gigantic hot-air balloon. William felt the current tugging at his tail. Alarmed, he shot to the surface, like the cork from a champagne bottle, and clung to a rock, his heart beating rapidly. Zeus rose beside him.

"What was *that*?!" William squealed, pointing downwards.

"Charybdis," whispered Zeus.

"You told me Charybdis was a whirlpool, not a monster," William exclaimed loudly.

"Sssssh!" hissed Zeus.

"Well, you did!" shouted William.

"It hardly seemed relevant," replied Zeus quietly. "The whirlpool she creates when drinking is the thing to be avoided. Whereas Scylla—"

Suddenly a snake's head – as large as William's human body – slashed through the air, cutting off Zeus mid-sentence. At once, the king of the gods dived, and the snake missed biting him by millimetres before it swung back to where it had come from. William looked up and was horrified by the sight that met his eyes. Serpents' heads had begun to spill from the cave in the cliffs above him like sinister spaghetti. He didn't want to think about what kind of body they might be attached to, but clearly there was nothing aged or retiring about this monster. The air was suddenly thick with coiling necks and thrashing heads and razor-sharp fangs. William stared, frozen, mouth agape in terror.

Athene was squawking, "Dive, William! Dive!" He was just about to follow Zeus when one of the heads snapped at Athene and caught the end of her tail feathers in its mouth. It swung her round and round and then flipped her into the air, throwing its head back as if she were a peanut to be swallowed whole.

With a heroic burst of tail flapping, William launched himself skywards, snatching Athene as he arced in an elegant curve over the massed heads of Scylla. He felt a rush of cold breath on his skin as jaws snapped at him. When he re-entered the water there was a loud clunk.

Fangs closed upon the bellows and William was jerked backwards. A horrible crunch was followed by a monstrous roar as the serpent tasted not soft, salty sea nymph, but hard, flavourless metal.

The beast dropped him, shaking its head from side to side in disgust. William dived deep, swam hard and resurfaced a couple of hundred metres away, out of striking distance.

He watched the many-headed beast withdraw grumpily back into its clifftop cave, and sighed with relief as the last forked tongue disappeared from view. Then he heard a small gasp and looked down. He had forgotten for a moment that he was still holding Athene.

The goddess was soggy and breathless but otherwise unharmed. Fortunately for William, she was so paralysed with gratitude that she was – for the time being at any rate – rendered speechless. Perching her on his golden locks so that her wings could dry out, William cruised through the waves with his head above water.

"Are the bellows OK?" he asked Zeus anxiously. "They're not punctured, are they?"

"No," replied Zeus. "Hephaestus's craftsmanship

is very sturdy. That's the least of our worries." Zeus sighed, and William noticed that his brow was furrowed with concern. "I'm beginning to wonder if this was wise," he said. "These bodies … swimming to England. It's all taking too long. We've still got the length of Italy to go up. Then there's France and the whole of Spain to get round. It's already Wednesday. At this rate we won't get to the Channel in time."

"Can't you summon Pegasus?"

"Why?"

"He could fly us there, couldn't he?" asked William.

Zeus regarded him sternly. "How on earth do you think a sea nymph could ride a horse?"

"Side-saddle?" ventured William.

"Too slippery," said Zeus. "No, it's impossible, I'm afraid. I suppose we shall just have to swim through the night. It might not be enough even then, but at least we shall have tried."

Anxiety began to settle upon them, making the water seem heavy and the going slow. William turned things over in his mind as he swam, Odysseus's words echoing in his ears. When they'd first met, his ancestor had told him, "Despair is the enemy… There is always *something* that can be done."

There must be some way they could speed themselves up. He just had to think of it, that was all. What did he do when he was late for school? Nip through Mrs Backwell's garden when she wasn't looking…

"Isn't there a short cut?" he wondered aloud.

Zeus stopped dead. So did William. Athene's claws dug into his head in alarm.

"A what?"

"A short cut across France. I don't know… Can't we go up a river or something?"

"Rivers flow *into* the sea, William, not in the other direction. If we swim up one of those we'll end up stranded in some mountain stream."

"OK, not a river, then." He thought again. His gran had been on a narrow boat holiday last Easter. William had been bored to tears by having to look at all the photos she'd taken. But now it could just be the answer. He was pretty sure his gran had been in France – that she'd gone all the way from one coast to the other…

"A canal," said William slowly. "That's what we need."

"A what?" asked Zeus.

"A canal. It's like a man-made river. People used them for carting stuff about in the olden days. France is full of them."

"Really?"

"Yes," said William, with more confidence than he felt.

"Mmm," considered Zeus. "If we can go through France we'll save a lot of time. Nice idea, William."

When they finally reached the French coast, they sent Athene to scout ahead and look for a possible entry route. She had just returned with news of a broad channel heading inland about a kilometre away when things got a whole lot more complicated.

Athene squawked and pointed with the tip of one white wing. William looked, and was appalled to see a huge wave rushing towards them. A tidal wave as big as a house ... a block of flats ... a mountain! And with a great crest that rippled in the sunshine like a horse's mane.

William rubbed his eyes and stared. It *was* a horse's mane. Several horses' manes, in fact. Only these horses didn't have any back legs, they had fishes' tails. And they were pulling a pearl-studded chariot in which a brine-encrusted, bearded figure heaved on the reins. In a swirl of frothing foam, the chariot slid to a halt beside Zeus and William.

"Oh, dear god," muttered Zeus, his rosy lips paling to a deathly white. "It's Poseidon."

POSEIDON

"Well, hello," crooned Poseidon. It was the kind of voice that William's mum would have called chocolatey, and William knew that it would have made her go all soppy. It didn't have that effect on him. His flesh crawled, and it took all his willpower not to swim as fast as he could in the opposite direction.

"I heard that some nymphs had crossed the Adriatic. Where have you two lovelies been hiding all my life?"

Zeus hissed to William, "I'll distract him. As soon as you get the chance, go with Athene. I'll catch you up later." He turned and, winding a curl of his golden tresses around one finger, looked coyly at Poseidon and attempted to arrange his lips into an appealing pout.

"We're not from these parts, your highness. We're down from the North Sea. Erm ... on holiday."

"Oh really? Tourists, huh? And how do you like the Mediterranean?"

"Very nice. Lovely and warm."

"And where have you been so far?"

"Oh ... here and there, your highness." Zeus's voice was as high and screechy as a pantomime dame's.

"Here and there, eh?" Poseidon chuckled. "Here and there. Well, you've been *there*, and now you're *here*." He twirled his seaweed moustache and said in a deeper voice, "And so am I."

Zeus flicked his curls casually over one shoulder and opened his eyes wide. "So you are."

110

"What do you say we get to know each other a little? You and your companion—"

"My niece," Zeus interrupted smoothly.

"Pretty little thing, isn't she?" Poseidon looked at William, and William knew that if he'd still had toes, they would have been curling with embarrassment.

"Pretty ... yes," said Zeus, pushing his "relative" behind him and saying to Poseidon in a low, confidential tone, "but she's no fun at all. Not like me." He rippled his tail and said, "You've a terrible reputation, your mightiness. They say no sea nymph's safe when you're about."

"Is that right?"

"Can it be true?" Zeus was fluttering his eyelashes frantically.

"Don't believe a word of it. You'll be safe in my hands."

"Oh really?"

"Come, sit beside me, and I'll prove it to you."

"All the way up there, your mightiness? In your great chariot? Oh, I couldn't."

"You could."

"I couldn't."

"You could."

111

"I couldn't."

William was beginning to wonder how long this was going to go on, and how he could possibly manage to slip away, when Zeus twirled his finger in his hair and said, "Oh, go on, then. I trust you."

Poseidon's answering chuckle was so loud that William could feel it vibrate right through his tail. It stunned several nearby fish who floated to the surface and lay there gawping helplessly.

Zeus swam slowly over to the chariot and held out a hand. "Pull me up, then, your mightiness," he said.

Poseidon reached out and took the nymph's hand. But, to his surprise, Zeus tugged so hard that the sea god was jerked from his chariot and came splashing down into the waves.

In the confusion, Zeus yelled, "Go! Swim, William, swim!"

William obeyed instantly, turning tail and heading for the shoreline in a frantic turmoil of foam and thrashing water. Athene, clinging to his hair, was flapping desperately as if she was trying to tug him along. He didn't stop until he had reached the entrance to a very murky canal and was heading inland. Only when he found his way blocked by a large lock did William pause for breath and reflect on the last, chilling words he'd heard the sea god speak: *"William?* Did you say 'William'? That's a very odd name for a sea nymph..."

William's short cut through the French canal system didn't prove as short as he'd hoped. First, there was the problem with locks. To get through he had to hang about waiting for boats to arrive and then sneak in, submerged, trying to avoid being sliced up by propellers or squished between the vessels that crowded into each lock. Then there was the problem of water quality. It was so murky that William found it hard to see underwater. But if he swam on the surface – keeping his tail well down so it wouldn't get spotted – there was the danger of people talking to him. In French.

Waving, gesticulating, demanding to know what he was up to. For a long time he swam from boat to boat as if he was simply a foolish holiday-maker who'd decided to take a quick dip. He'd gone several miles like this when he grumbled to Athene, "I wish I'd brought some Lethe water with me."

"Oh!" she said, perching on his head. "How silly of me! I can do that!" With a loud belch, she trickled warm water on his head.

Now William could cruise – if not unnoticed, at least unremembered – through the waterways of France.

Like his ancestor Odysseus, William had no sense of direction so he had to rely on Athene who flew high above, checking the network, swooping down whenever William needed to fork left or right into a different canal.

But he still couldn't build up the speed he would have liked to maintain. If he thrashed his tail too energetically he stirred up the water so that waves crashed against the sides of the canal and bounced back, throwing him off balance. His swim was more of a stroll than a sprint. Worse, he was hungry.

He managed to chomp down a couple of trout, but river fish tasted oddly muddy in comparison to the sardines he'd consumed in the sea, and their skins were slimy and unappealing. He kept having to swim past boats where people were barbecuing burgers or breaking open baguettes and spreading them with creamy, garlicy cheese. Hunger made him miserable and tired so he slowed down even more. By the time the sun set he was hardly moving and so exhausted that he barely managed to pull himself up onto the bank to sleep.

That night, William tossed and turned and dozed – his stomach grumbling painfully – under a weeping willow somewhere in southern France. At dawn, he set off once more.

He hadn't gone far when he came across the remains of a discarded picnic floating in the canal. William tore open the bag and crammed soggy sandwiches, squished grapes, a bruised banana and a half-eaten cake into his mouth until his stomach stopped its noisy protest.

Refreshed, he swam on. And on. And on. He swam through the crowded canals for the whole, long day, wondering what had happened to Zeus and how on earth he was going to cope with the kraken if the king of the gods didn't catch up with him.

It wasn't until William reached Paris that night that he heard a familiar call and turned to see Zeus surging towards him. William smiled with relief, but the king of the gods was looking strangely uncomfortable.

"You OK?" asked William.

"I don't wish to discuss it," answered Zeus shortly.

That was fine with William. He had plenty of other things to worry about. Like getting through Paris. In the dark, it was a complete nightmare – after a tricky series of locks, the canal had merged into the River Seine which was choked with pleasure boats giving loud, aquatic tours of the city to tourists of every nationality. Recorded commentaries blared across the water and made it hard to hear Athene's directions.

Whenever William accidentally took a mouthful of the water it tasted vile, and there were all kinds of nasty objects littering the river bed which he kept crashing into.

But at last they were out of the urban sprawl, back in the canal system and heading north through farmland. Eventually William caught a whiff of the sea, a tang of salt in the brackish water.

"The coast's getting near," he said excitedly.

"So's the kraken," replied Zeus darkly.

It was Friday morning. They had swum through the entire night. As dawn lit the cold grey water with an equally cold grey light, the two sea nymphs emerged into the English Channel.

THE KRAKEN

William was tired and hungry, and the straps that held the bellows on his back were rubbing his shoulders raw. But he couldn't rest or eat. Somewhere in that expanse of chilly water lurked a sleepy kraken. He was going to have to find it, and fast.

"Where do we start?" he asked Zeus.

"No idea," was the far from comforting reply.

William supposed that the obvious thing was to swim towards England. For once he didn't have any problem finding the way. They were in the middle of a shipping lane with ferries chugging from France to England. As long as they kept one within sight, William knew they were heading in the right direction.

Very soon, they were nearing Dover. William could see the famous white cliffs – more of a dingy puce that particular morning – in the distance.

They paused and watched the ferry they had been following dock in the busy port and start to unload. Almost immediately a different vessel set off, heading in their direction.

At that moment there was a quivering tremble deep in the Channel. A bubble rose to the surface beside William as if something very large had farted deep in the water below. Zeus looked at him and tutted, "*Really*, William!"

"It wasn't me!" he protested.

Another bubble rose and popped beside Zeus.

"See?" said William.

Zeus frowned. "Ah," he said. "Well, we seem to have located the kraken, at any rate. It must be somewhere down there."

A steady stream of bubbles began to rise, making the surface churn and foam. William suddenly found he had to flap his tail hard to keep his head above water – the sea seemed to have thinned already. It wasn't holding him up properly any more.

In panic, he turned and saw Zeus was having the same problem. And then Athene started squawking, "Look out! LOOK OUT!!!"

The approaching ferry was coming at them fast. But before it could hit them head on, it lurched heavily sideways, missing them by millimetres.

As it passed, the boat righted itself but then lurched hard in the other direction. William stared, horrified. The vessel was pitching and rolling like the little plastic boat in the museum. Only this boat had people on it – a lot of people – and they were screaming as they were tossed about the decks.

William knew exactly what would happen next. The sea would be unable to support the weight of the ship and it would sink, taking all its passengers with it.

With a fierce effort in the rapidly thinning water, William hurled himself at the ferry like a speeding torpedo. Zeus was beside him and there was a resounding clang as they banged into the metal hull.

"We need to get it back to shore!" shouted William.

"Fine," said Zeus, his teeth clenched with concentration.

William's logical mind told him that no one could push a ferry. But it seemed sea nymphs had surprising reserves of strength. Together they drove the vessel before them with such force that, when it re-entered the harbour, it caused a small tidal wave to wash over the cars that had been parked there, ready to take the next crossing. The ship crashed against the dock and every astonished passenger fell over.

The ferry was rescued.

The British Isles were not.

When William – gasping for breath – looked up at the white cliffs, they seemed to tilt. Just a little. For a moment, he thought his vision had gone funny: the effort of pushing the ferry must have dizzied him. He blinked hard and stared up at the cliffs once more. They looked as they always did on postcards. But then it happened again. William watched the white cliffs tilt very slightly sideways.

And then they began to wobble.

"The kraken's moved! It must be going under the land to settle down!" shouted Zeus. "We need to be quick, William."

Zeus disappeared beneath the waves. Taking a very deep breath he hoped wouldn't be his last, William dived after him.

The Channel wasn't as muddy as a canal, or as full of rubbish as the river in Paris, but it was still pretty murky. It took a while for William's eyes to adjust to the gloom.

He looked nervously about him but all he could see was the silty bottom of the sea. When he peered shorewards he noticed that it shelved gradually upwards until it reached the beach. And yet Zeus said the kraken had gone under the land. Where? How? He looked at the king of the gods, puzzled, and saw he was pointing in the opposite direction.

"This is the way, I believe," Zeus said, his voice sounding strange and distorted underwater. "We have to head out to sea a little before we can get under."

William followed, and they swam further out into the Channel. Below them, what William had taken to be the bottom of the sea sloped and then suddenly stopped, dead. It wasn't the real sea bed: it was merely a bit of submerged land at the edge of the British Isles. Where it ended, the water became immensely dark. The real sea bed must be far, far below. As they swam deeper, William could see that the land was like a huge floating raft, perched precariously on a couple of spindly columns. It cut out all light from the sun so the water was colder and murkier than ever and it was impossible to see far ahead.

It wasn't until William struck something dense and rubbery – hitting it with such gusto that he rebounded for several metres – that he knew they'd found the creature they were looking for.

He'd expected something enormous, but nothing had prepared him for this. He touched the top of a tentacle and ran his hand along it to estimate its length. He'd swum more than fifty metres when he realized he was nowhere near the end – the thing hadn't even begun to taper to a point. The creature was beyond big; beyond vast. William knew at once he didn't have enough words in his brain to cover the scale of the beast he had to wake.

And what was he armed with? A few litres of cold coffee. William's plan suddenly seemed stupid. Pointless. Doomed to fail. He swallowed the lump that had risen in his throat. Told himself sternly to get on with it before the steady stream of bubbles upended the British Isles and sent them sliding to the floor of the ocean like a plate dropped sideways into a sink.

The problem was that William had no idea how to find the creature's mouth. He supposed it was where all the bubbles were coming from, but they were now blasting so forcefully that he risked being carried away in the jetstream. If he squirted coffee into that, it would be washed away instantly and diluted in the depths of the Channel.

"We've got to wake it up," said William.

"I know," said Zeus.

"I mean now. Just for a second, so I can find its mouth. I can't get the coffee into it otherwise."

"That's dangerous, William. Very dangerous."

"I know. There's no other way."

But it seemed that the beast was a deep sleeper. They bounced on what they assumed to be its head, they pinched its suckers, they tweaked the pointy tips of every tentacle, but nothing roused it.

The land above had started tipping badly. At that moment a car – fortunately empty – sailed past them on the strong current and disappeared into the blackness. It was followed by another. And another. They were coming thick and fast as the entire contents of a harbourside car park slid into the sea.

Watching the cars glide past gave William an idea. As one narrowly missed him, he broke off its aerial and swam to the kraken. He found a softish, roundish bit of its body and, grasping the aerial firmly, gave it a good, hard poke.

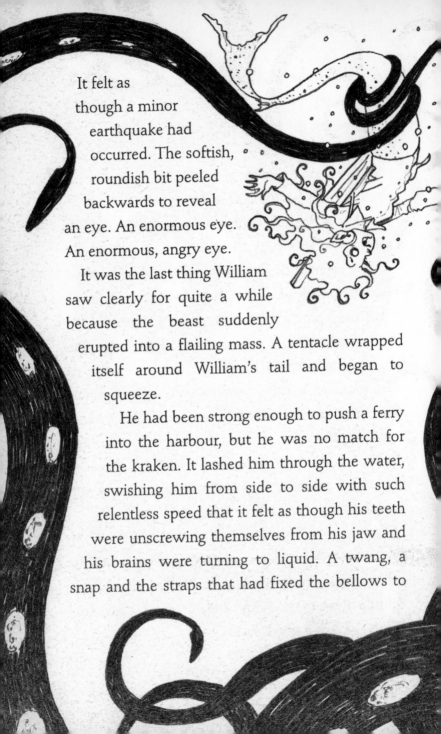

It felt as though a minor earthquake had occurred. The softish, roundish bit peeled backwards to reveal an eye. An enormous eye. An enormous, angry eye.

It was the last thing William saw clearly for quite a while because the beast suddenly erupted into a flailing mass. A tentacle wrapped itself around William's tail and began to squeeze.

He had been strong enough to push a ferry into the harbour, but he was no match for the kraken. It lashed him through the water, swishing him from side to side with such relentless speed that it felt as though his teeth were unscrewing themselves from his jaw and his brains were turning to liquid. A twang, a snap and the straps that had fixed the bellows to

his back on the long journey from Mount Olympus gave way. The bellows – and the precious coffee inside – sank into the gloomy depths. All was lost.

But then there was Zeus. William could hear him shouting at the kraken, "Let him go, you great ugly cephalopod!"

It worked. The creature was distracted. It didn't release William, but it relaxed its hold for a fraction of a second – long enough for him to wriggle free and speed in the direction the bellows had fallen.

He could hear Zeus behind him. "Take that, you filthy great squid!"

William didn't know what Zeus had hit it with, but there was a roar. He looked up, and for the first time he could see the creature's mouth. It gaped wide, looming above his head – a churning mass of muscle to suck prey inside and slowly squeeze it to death. But its mouth wasn't aiming for William. An unearthly, eerie gurgling shook the ocean, and the creature sped past him.

An even eerier silence followed. Zeus was nowhere to be seen, and the kraken was letting out a monstrous belch.

William was appalled. But he didn't have time for

regrets. Zeus had become a meal for the monster. And what did grown-ups have to round off a nice meal? Coffee!

There was nothing for it but to dive. Deeper and deeper into the dense blackness. And just as he was despairing of ever finding the bellows, a glint of gold caught his eye. William dashed towards it, blindly snatching with both hands. They were still full – still intact. He turned, unscrewing the silver cap as he swam rapidly up towards the kraken. He was dizzied by being tossed around, and now lack of oxygen was slowing him down. His brain fuzzily tried to work out how to find the creature's mouth. He supposed he was going to have to let himself be eaten, just like Zeus. He hoped it would be quick. Painless.

But then a thought stirred somewhere in his mind. He paused, looking at the bellows. The end was sharp. Pointed. It reminded him of something... He barely had time to think as a tentacle curled itself around his waist and he was carried, unresistingly, towards the kraken's mouth.

Suddenly a light switched itself on in William's brain. The pointy end was like a syringe! And

syringes were used for injections... He lifted the
bellows and, with the last of his strength, plunged
the point into the tentacle that held him. As he
brought the handles together, pure, undiluted coffee
shot straight into the creature's bloodstream.

Face to face with the kraken, William could see
its eyes widening so far, they looked as though
they might pop clean out of its head. A million

volts seemed to pass through it as its many tentacles were flung out with such electric energy that William was thrown far out into the Channel, and the golden bellows were lost to the deep.

Bobbing to the surface, William took a gasping breath of sweet air.

A moment later, the kraken too bobbed up to the surface, its limbs sticking out as stiff and rigid as the quills of a sea urchin. It spiralled – gigantic, spectacular – revolving slowly in the current, and William wondered guiltily if the coffee had killed it.

But then it roused itself, wide awake, fully alert and very hungry. It looked at William. Reached a tentacle towards him…

But before it wrapped itself around him, the kraken went cross-eyed. Its head bulged. Shivering, it flushed blue, then red, then purple, then orange. Suddenly it released a vast cloud of what William assumed was squiddy ink that turned the entire Channel filthy brown and smelt *appalling*. Then the kraken was off, diving deep, and heading for the warmer waters of Bermuda.

RETURN TO SPITFLOS

Exhausted, William floated on the surface of the sea, staring up at the sky and wondering what to do. He supposed he ought to feel pleased with himself. He ought to be delighted that his idea had worked. He'd saved the British Isles. And Europe. Not bad for a ten-year-old boy. He should have felt smug with triumph, but somehow he couldn't summon up enough energy for even a little smirk.

The kraken had gone. But so had Zeus. And the world seemed cold and small and grey without him.

There was a flutter of white and Athene swooped down to perch on his head. For once he was glad to see her – it was nice to have some company. Or so he thought. But then she spoke.

Looking at William and the expanse of filthy brown water, she asked, "Where's Daddy?"

William sighed. "He got eaten."

"Eaten?!" she gasped.

"'Fraid so."

"Oh my goodness! How terrible! What are you going to do?"

"I don't know."

"Daddy's gone!" she wailed. "Poor Daddy!" She pecked William crossly on the head. And then she added, "That sea nymph was Hera's best body. She's going to be furious with you."

"Me?"

"Yes ... well, this was your plan, wasn't it?"

Athene sniffed. "So, clearly, you're the one to blame. Oh dear. It's not nice having Hera as an enemy, I can assure you."

"Great," said William dully. His favourite god was deep in the belly of some sea monster, and now both Poseidon and Hera were his arch enemies. Things didn't look too bright. He was going to have to swim back to Spitflos and retrieve his body all alone. It was such a long journey, and he was so tired. Suddenly it all seemed too much. William hung his head, took a deep breath and prepared to cry.

Just then he felt the water stir beneath him. For a moment, he thought it was the kraken coming back to swallow him for pudding. But then, shooting out of the sea in a great triumphal arc, came Zeus. Slimy, begrimed with brown sludge, his golden hair a wreckage on his head ... but alive and in one piece.

"Daddy! Daddy! Daddy!" screeched Athene.

If he hadn't smelt quite so bad, William might have hugged him. As it was, he held his nose, breathing in through his mouth, and asked, "How did you manage to escape?"

Zeus was scraping his hair frantically, trying to rid himself of the mucky slime. "It seems coffee has some surprising side effects, William."

"Like what?"

"It turns out to be a rather efficient purgative."

"A what?" asked William.

"A laxative," said Zeus. "I was whooshed through that creature's digestive system at high speed. Barely touched the sides."

"You mean you came out of its—"

"No need to go into details," interrupted Zeus. "Suffice to say I have emerged intact."

William's brain was ticking over. He thought back to the kraken's astonished expression, and to the vast cloud of brown stuff that it had suddenly ejected. "Hang on," he said. "That wasn't ink, was it?"

"No," replied Zeus. "It wasn't."

William looked at the dirty, smelly water all around him and suddenly, without a word, began swimming very fast towards the coast of France. He didn't want to hang about in a cloud of kraken poo for a moment longer than was necessary.

*   *   *

135

They found a sheltered spot beneath a clump of trees that overhung the canal, and there all three of them rested. William slept deeply, despite the hardness of the ground, and woke feeling both refreshed and hungry.

"I could catch you some mice," offered Athene. "Warm and fresh? Make a lovely meal. How about it?"

"Er ... no thanks," said William.

He had to make do with half the slippery trout that Zeus had caught and a crust of soggy baguette that someone had thrown in the water for the ducks. They weren't very pleased to find a sea nymph competing for their food, and William received several nasty pecks before he wrestled the bread away from them.

The journey back was long and weary. They edged slowly around the coast of Italy, squeezing carefully and silently between Scylla and Charybdis. When they got close to the sirens, William swam with his fingers stuck firmly in his ears.

By Sunday, they were back in Spitflos. The sight of the island – bleached from emerald green to palest brown by the heat of summer, with its little town spilling down the side of the mountain like milk from a jug – filled William with delight. He was tired, he was hungry, but he was home.

They reached the cove just before sunset and hid behind the rocks until the last tourists left the beach. When the sand was finally empty, they flipped and wriggled their way inelegantly across to the cave where Hera and Artemis had stashed their bodies.

Zeus picked up the flattened swan shape and smoothed it out beside him. "It wasn't as much fun as I thought, being a sea nymph," he said. "Between you and me, William, I shall be relieved to get back into this."

As William watched, the sea nymph deflated like a Lilo whose stopper had been removed, and the swan puffed up, swelling and growing until Zeus was back to his old self once more.

"There'll be trouble on Mount Olympus over this," commented Zeus as he rolled up the grubby body. "I don't suppose the hair will ever be quite the same again. The rows will go on for aeons, I expect. Ah well, can't be helped. There's always a price to be paid for saving the world, eh, William?" The bald swan gave what would have been a reassuring smile – if swans could bend their beaks. "Your turn, William," he said. "Do you need help to change?"

William didn't answer. He was raking the floor of the darkening cavern with increasing panic, but in the pit of his stomach he already knew it was hopeless.

William's body had vanished.

POSEIDON'S REVENGE

A deep chuckle rolled across the water from far out at sea, like a distant rumble of thunder. Before he'd even lifted his head, William knew that it was Poseidon. Silhouetted against the sinking sun he could make out the shape of his human body dangling from the sea god's outstretched hand.

"William Popidopolis, descendant of Odysseus the villainous cur, I have it!" he roared. "I shall take this in revenge for what was done to my son."

William noticed with alarm that the colour had drained away from Zeus's pimpled flesh and the swan glowed an unnatural white in the fading light. "Oh dear," whispered the king of the gods. "Now you're in trouble."

"What's he after?" asked William.

"He's going to punish you for Odysseus blinding the Cyclops," twittered Athene.

"That's not fair!" exclaimed William. "It was years ago. And it was nothing to do with me."

"That hardly matters, I'm afraid," said Zeus grimly. "The blood of Odysseus runs in your veins. He doesn't care which generation it comes from, as long as some of it gets spilt."

A loud grating echoed across the bay. William couldn't see what Poseidon was doing, but it sounded horribly like the sea god was sharpening a knife.

"Can't you order him to give it back?" begged William.

"Unfortunately not. I have no power in Poseidon's

realm. I shouldn't even have been there, really, it's against the rules. I was hoping he wouldn't find out."

"Rules?" protested William. "But you're the king of the gods!"

"Even immortals have to follow rules. It's only polite. If I go against them we'll be sunk into a state of chaos, and we can't have that again."

"Look on the bright side," said Athene. "It's only your body he's taken. I'm sure Hera won't mind if you keep that one."

"I don't want to be stuck as a mermaid!"

"Sea nymph," corrected Athene.

"Whatever," growled William. He was furious. He'd swum across half of Europe and back, fought a sea monster, saved a continent and this was his thanks – being trapped inside a body with a fishy tail and a shell bikini top. For ever. He'd had enough.

"I'm going to get it back," he snarled.

"What?" squawked Athene.

"My body." He started to flop seawards, ungainly as a walrus but twice as menacing. He heard the cries of Athene and Zeus fading as he propelled himself out to sea, but he wasn't listening to their protests. He'd spent ten years in that small frame: he couldn't sit still and let Poseidon do whatever he wanted with it.

By now it was almost dark. William swam with determined speed towards the sea god. He was entirely alone. Whatever happened next was down to him.

He drew level with Poseidon's chariot, narrowly missing the sea horses' thrashing hooves and swishing tails. He saw with a sinking heart that he was right – Poseidon had sharpened his knife and was now pointing it at his deflated body.

"That's mine!" yelled William. "And I want it back."

Poseidon turned and looked at him. He smiled – a cold, leering grin of malice. "Oh you do, do you?"

"Yes."

The sea god's voice dropped to a low sneer. "Then come and get it."

Without warning, Poseidon

reached down and
grabbed William
by the tail, flick-
ing him up and
into the chariot,
like a cat hooking
a goldfish out of a
bowl. He looked at
him and laughed
aloud. William had the
sinking sensation that
he'd played right into the sea god's hands.
Poseidon had meant for him to come out where
Zeus couldn't help him.

William had the sensation of being a tube of
toothpaste all over again. It was dark. He couldn't
see exactly how it happened, but he could feel
himself being squeezed and squashed until he was
as thin as a length of sticky string being drawn out
through his nostril. A moment's suspension in the
salty air, and then he felt comfortable – deliciously
comfortable – apart from the pins and needles in
his right toe.

His toe? His toe! He had feet! Complete with

trainers! Legs, lovely legs, instead of a flappy tail. William felt his head. There it was – his hair, short and curling wildly like it should be. He whooped, exhilarated with sheer joy, only to be crushed by Poseidon's chilling voice informing him, "Now you shall die."

Poseidon hadn't wanted to kill an empty body – what would be the point? He'd lured William out just so he could murder him properly.

William couldn't fight a god. It was impossible. But at least he didn't have to be a sea nymph for the rest of his life. And he'd end up in Elysium. It would be a bit sooner than he'd hoped, but at least he knew it was nice there. They had that Wish Fulfilment Programme to keep the dead heroes amused. He could play in the World Cup and score the winning goal every day for all eternity if he wanted. And he'd be with Odysseus. He could teach his ancestor to play football too. There should be enough Greek heroes down there to make a couple of teams. Resigned to his fate, William said, "Go on, then."

"Pardon?" said Poseidon.

His mum would be upset, William realized.

Mind you, she might not even remember she had a son after all the Lethe water Zeus had slipped her. Perhaps Zeus could keep her topped up with it. She wouldn't have to be upset at all then—

"I SAID, 'PARDON?'" repeated Poseidon crossly.

"What?" asked William. "Oh... I said, 'Go on, then.' Go on ... do it." Helpfully, William lifted up his chin, exposing his neck.

Poseidon frowned. "Aren't you going to make a fuss?"

"No," replied William.

"What ... no weeping?"

"No."

"No wailing?"

"No."

"No gnashing?"

"What?" asked William.

"Gnashing," explained Poseidon. "Of teeth. Very effective if you want to express wild and desperate sorrow."

"Oh," said William. "Well, I wouldn't know how to. Gnash them, I mean. So, no, thank you."

Poseidon pouted sulkily. "How disappointing." He shifted irritably on his seaweedy seat. "It's no fun without the weeping and wailing and gnashing of teeth. I mean, where's the satisfaction in smiting someone without that? Makes it all rather pointless. Are you sure you don't want to do it?"

"Quite sure."

"Just a bit? To please me?"

"No, thank you."

Poseidon stuck his bottom lip out moodily. "Without the cringing and whining it all seems a bit dull. I need to get worked up if I'm to squish a contemptible mortal. How can I do that if you're not behaving contemptibly? You're making me feel like a bully."

William folded his arms across his chest but said nothing. He fixed Poseidon with a frank, fearless stare, and before him the sea god seemed to shrink.

"I suppose it was a long time ago..." said Poseidon.

William raised an eyebrow. He said nothing.

The sea god's patience snapped. He seized William in a mighty hand and threw him high into the air. As William came back down, Poseidon did something like a handstand in his chariot.

He swung his enormous tail, thwacking William shorewards as if he were a golf ball.

As William landed on the soft sand of Spitflos and the distant chariot of Poseidon sank beneath the waves, he could just make out the sea god's reluctant departing words: "William Popidopolis, I must sadly confess that my brother was right. You are indeed a hero."

William hardly remembered the journey back to Brighton, not because he'd drunk Lethe water but because he was so tired. Zeus had offered to take him to Mount Olympus for ambrosia and a good sleep, but he'd had enough of the squabbling gods: he wanted to go home. And so Pegasus had flown late into the night, William dozing fitfully with his nose resting on the horse's mane, being savagely pecked awake by Zeus every time he started to slip sideways.

Pegasus landed in his garden well after midnight, where William briefly noted that the bathroom window was unmended. Inside, Kate was still up and about, staring at things vacantly as if she couldn't quite recall who she was or what she was supposed to be doing.

"It should wear off soon," promised Zeus. "A couple of days and everything will be fine."

Athene, eyes shiny with tears, blinked furiously. Finding herself utterly speechless, she flew off in a flurry of white feathers.

Zeus fixed William with his piercing blue eyes. "Goodbye, William Popidopolis," he said. "You have proved yourself once again. A hero whose courage knows no bounds, neither on land nor sea. Well done."

Pegasus stretched his wings and they were gone.

Throat aching, William waved until the flying horse disappeared from view. And then, tucking himself into his nice, warm, comfortable bed, he fell into a deep, deep sleep.

When William woke up, things were back to normal. Almost.

It was Monday morning. Again. Yawning wearily, William dressed, gave his mum a shout and was answered by the gloriously familiar wail: "Coffeeeeee... Pleeeeeeease ... neeeeeed coffeeeeeeeee, Wiiiiiiiiill..."

Over breakfast, Kate spread the newspaper on the table and said, horrified, "Look! All sorts of dreadful things have been happening! A ferry was hit by these weird fish-shaped torpedos in the Channel – driven clean back into the docks! And there was a dreadful sewage spill too. Really nasty. Eeuw! The whole Channel turned brown. And it says here that temporary amnesia has been affecting the entire population of south-east England! Everyone's been wandering around being vague and forgetful. Something odd in the water, apparently. The government are going to sue. That explains a lot. I wondered why I felt so funny. I can't remember a thing about the last few days, can you?"

William smiled to himself. He thought of the quarrelsome gods; the sirens; the monsters; the kraken; Poseidon. The last few days had been frightening and exhausting and very, very weird. But one thing was certain: he wasn't ever likely to forget them.

William Popidopolis is in a race against time!

Has William got to Greece in time to help Zeus retie the knot that secures the world? He may be a god, but the bossy swan urgently needs William's help.

BY TANYA LANDMAN

When she was ten years old, Katrina Picket woke Merlin. It was quite by accident – she'd had no intention of doing any such thing. But it was fortunate for everyone in England that she did. They didn't know, of course. The whole thing had to be hushed up. Most people thought it was a particularly inventive party for the Queen's jubilee. And as for the dragon and the exploding fireball – they were explained away as impressive special effects.

But Katrina, and the Prime Minister, knew different...

"Fast-moving fun." *The Scotsman*

BY TANYA LANDMAN

It's Katrina Picket's birthday, and not only has her favourite bear been burnt to a crisp, but her best friend's ignoring her and their supply teacher is none other than Morgan le Fay, the most evil sorceress that ever lived! Katrina summons Merlin. But can he train her to become a sorceress in time to defeat Morgan and save the country from destruction?

BY TANYA LANDMAN

High above the mountain village of Fracture, trouble is brewing. The sorceress Lady Lamorna has her heart set on a new robe. To get it she will stop at nothing, including kidnapping, blackmail and more than a little black magic. But she reckons without the heroic Gracie Gillypot, not to mention a gallant if rather scruffy prince, two chatty bats, the wickedest stepsister ever, a troll with a grudge – and some very Ancient Crones.

An exuberant, fast-moving and wildly entertaining tale, with a cast of characters who are good, bad and very, very ugly, *The Robe of Skulls* will enthral all those who like their stories a little bit different.

BY VIVIAN FRENCH

**If you've enjoyed reading this book,
look out for...**

Short novels for fluent readers